RESET DAY

RESET DAY

BY **CARLY ANNE WEST**
ART BY **TIM HEITZ** AND **ARTFUL DOODLERS**

Scholastic Inc.

All rights reserved. Published by Scholastic Inc., *Publishers since 1920.* SCHOLASTIC and associated logos are trademarks and/or registered trademarks of Scholastic Inc.

The publisher does not have any control over and does not assume any responsibility for author or third-party websites or their content.

This book is a work of fiction. Names, characters, places, and incidents are either the product of the author's imagination or are used fictitiously, and any resemblance to actual persons, living or dead, business establishments, events, or locales is entirely coincidental.

Library of Congress Cataloging-in-Publication Data available

ISBN 978-1-338-71740-2

1 2021

Printed in the U.S.A. 23

First printing 2021

Book design by Cheung Tai

PROLOGUE

The lights are so bright, they give Bruce a headache.

"Tell me again," his coworker, Hal, says, "why we're pretending like it's the 1800s? Don't we have machines that can drill for us?"

Bruce watches Hal look longingly at the unused excavator and jackhammer on the ground. Bruce looks at it, too, but only for a fleeting moment—the smallest, tiniest, most minuscule amount of time. Then they bring up their pickaxes again.

"It's called a noise ordinance, Hal, and I didn't invent it," Bruce grumbles. He's grumpy, though maybe more for having to explain it for the hundredth time to Hal. "At least we're getting time and a half."

"Time and a half, pah!" Hal spits. "We're working through the night with a toy hammer. Remind me to thank our genius union rep for negotiating such a sweet deal."

"Remind me to thank him for the overnight shift with *you*," Bruce quips, dragging his saw back and forth over the char-stained cement. Though as he chips away at the twenty-five-year-old concrete, he smells a familiar scent of burning wood. Bruce wagers he'll never understand what warranted destroying a perfectly good amusement park. But he's probably biased—after all, Bruce was always a sucker for a good tilt-a-whirl.

Then Bruce hears Hal sigh.

"There it is again," Hal says, raising his nose in the air to get a strong whiff of smoke.

"Just more of a reason to get through this as fast as possible," Bruce replies, continuing his work. Admittedly, he smelled the smoke before Hal, but he didn't want to say anything. Hal spooks easily, and Bruce didn't want to be the harder worker *and* the braver one . . . *but here we are.*

Hal shakes his head. "Those tunnels burned straight through decades ago. There's no way there are fires still going. Heck, there's no way there are tunnels at all anymore. Not here in Raven Brooks," he says.

Bruce is growing tired of Hal's rants. They never seem to end. But to Hal's credit, Bruce doesn't buy the underground fire story, either, not for one second. No, something else happened here . . . but Bruce isn't sure what. And at this point, maybe it's better he doesn't know.

"Look," says Hal, peering over each shoulder before leaning in closer to Bruce. "All I'm saying is that those theme-park people messed with things that shouldn't have been messed with. And somewhere along the line, things got evil. Real evil."

Bruce is silent.

"Kids *died*, Bruce," Hal finishes.

Bruce stifles the shiver he's been hiding under his collar all night. And it's not from the cold.

"C'mon, Hal, get a grip. It was a handful of rich people

running around with shiny rocks. They got in over their heads, then they got caught, end of story."

"Okay, so how do you explain Ted Peterson?" Hal challenges.

Bruce laughs. He can't help it. Ted Peterson? That nutty guy? "*Explain* Ted Peterson? I'm not sure anyone can 'explain' Ted Peterson."

But Hal isn't laughing, and pretty soon, Bruce is back to shrugging that chill from his spine.

"Peterson was worse than any of 'em," Bruce says, and he means it. But if he has any incriminating intel, he doesn't share.

Bruce and Hal continue working away, this time in silence. The smoke smell drifts in the air, but it's not what Bruce is thinking about right now. What exactly was that guy Peterson involved in? Was he really all that bad? Did he mean to kill those kids? And then . . .

"What if Ted Peterson's not gone?"

Bruce doesn't realize he says this question out loud.

As Bruce's own voice dawns on him, a low-flying crow swoops through the spotlight of their worksite, cawing. And then, like lightning, the earth below them begins to rumble and shake. Pieces of broken cement skitter around Bruce's and Hal's boots as they watch helplessly, each waiting for the other to assure them it's all in their heads.

"Bruce?" says Hal, with the ground still quivering beneath him.

Bruce points to Hal's feet. "Look out!"

But it's too late. Bruce can tell that Hal doesn't see the ground open like a gaping mouth. Nor does he smell the acrid air or feel the waft of heat rising from the cracked earth.

Bruce watches as the ground swallows Hal whole.

"HAL!" Bruce screams, rushing to the edge of the crater that's just formed, but a wave of heat forces him back and knocks him over, pulling him rolling down a nearby hill.

Bruce lands hard on a pile of concrete rubble before clambering back to the edge of the hole.

"Hal?" he calls out. "Hal? HAL? *HAAAL*?" Each call is filled with more desperation than before.

But Bruce's calling is in vain. A final, giant wave of blistering air rises to the crater's surface. It grabs hold of Bruce and drags him in.

As if on cue, the night sky gets darker. And the crow perches in a tree, watching it all unfold.

CHAPTER 1

"**A**re we there yet?" my sister, Delia, calls out as she kicks the back of my seat. She's asked this question maybe two hundred times since we got in the car on the drive to our new house, and if I hear her perky voice again—and feel her legs against the ridge of my back—I'll have no choice. I'll have to disown her.

"I don't know, but I'm going to need some serious massage therapy ASAP," I say, rubbing the spot where she punctured me through the seat.

"Pip, you're thirteen, not three hundred," replies Delia.

Mom, driving swiftly through some empty roundabout, realizes she has to play mediator.

"Girls, hold it together for another five minutes. We're almost there."

I groan. Mom has been saying "five more minutes" for the past hour. I won't admit it, but I agree with Delia. This road trip has taken *forever*.

I lean my head out the open window and feel the wind in my hair. The purple dye has faded to a lavender I actually like more, and it looks almost iridescent in the sun.

As Mom's car pushes on, the trees around grow thicker,

almost like we're entering a different part of the world. And I guess, in a way, we are. When I told my old friends I was moving to place called Raven Brooks, no one—including me—had ever heard of it. I put up a stink about moving, but then Mom said I could dye my hair if we did, and, well . . . you know the rest of that story.

"I think I made a wrong turn. Piper, weren't we on track near that forest preserve?" Mom says, chewing the fingernail on her index finger. She keeps asking me to check the map app on my phone, but it doesn't seem to recognize where we are, either.

The fading sun hits the tiny diamond on her wedding ring, and I swallow the knot that forms in my throat. Truth be told, my position as "road-trip navigator" is new—that was always Dad.

Dad isn't here anymore, I remind myself. *You've inherited the mantle.*

"Mom, that wasn't a road. That wasn't even a hiking trail," says Delia, and for the first time in over an hour, I don't argue with her.

After all, it's not Delia's fault. It's not Mom's, either. This whole mess isn't anyone's fault but the universe's.

Thanks, Universe.

I'm about to restart the map app for the eightieth time when Mom races by a signpost covered almost entirely by a massive tree branch.

"Mom, stop!" I screech.

In a move I don't think even she saw coming, Mom jams her

foot down on the break, lurching all three of us forward and skidding the car to a full stop in the middle of the road.

"What?" Mom demands.

"Uh, I think I saw a sign," I say meekly, and she eases back into the driver's seat, ignoring the tiny snort from Delia behind her.

"Sorry," I say. "I didn't realize you were so . . ."

"Exactly," Delia helps me out. "Nope. Not tense at all. Totally chill."

Mom reverses the car down the empty road.

There, as if hiding on purpose, is the back half of a sign. I can just barely make out the "RAV" above the "OKS" below it. But once I do, there's no mistaking it— that's the sign for Raven Brooks.

Mom stops the car so I can get out and move the tree vine in the way.

"Hmm," I say, peering at the sign.

"Get this. It says Raven Brooks: three hundred feet."

Mom shakes her head. "That's not possible."

I shrug and point up. "Tell that to the sign."

I have to admit, though—Mom's right. Three *hundred* feet? Surely we've been everywhere in that radius at this point. And it's all overgrown shrubbery.

Unless, a voice creeps in the back of my head, *it isn't?*

Mom sighs, her thousandth deep breath of our trip across three state lines. She sounds exhausted. I guess I would be, too. We only lost Dad a few months ago, and now we're moving, and on top of it all, she's got to deal with me and Delia. Mostly Delia, of course, but me, too. The very least the universe can offer her is an easy drive to our new home.

I climb back into the car. If I had any confidence that Raven Brooks really was three hundred feet ahead, I'd sprint the whole way, letting the thick July air coat my skin as I ran.

As we creep toward the three-hundred-foot mark, Mom slows the car to a near stop.

"There!" I yelp after several seconds of silent searching.

"Piper, are you sure?" Mom says, squinting into the thick spate of trees crowding the road's shoulder.

"Oh! I see it now," Delia says. "Just under the branch of that big, gnarly one."

She points to a tree suitable for any nightmare. It has that knotted-twisted-old-oak look that just screams *I've been here longer than you, and I'll outlive you five times over.*

"How on earth did you girls spot that?" Mom says, leaning over me to get a better look at the alleged road.

"It's Piper, remember?" says Delia, and I can practically hear her eyes rolling back into her head. "It's her superpower."

My superpower. I cringe at Delia's words, but she's not wrong. I have a talent that's useless 99.9 percent of the time—an ability to notice what others usually don't. Or, as Dad used to say, I have the devastatingly boring gift of "observation." Mom says I have an eye for detail, but Delia characterizes it the way only a little sister could: She calls me Eyeball, which is maybe the most disgusting name to give a sibling. Except for Nose Hair. That's the name I've blessed her with. (And you can probably guess why.) I win.

Mom cranks the wheel of the car and rolls us slowly over the crunchy foliage blanketing the road. Tree branches scrape the top of the car, making a spine-rattling screech with every pass underneath one of the old trees' claws.

"Bird," Delia says suddenly from the back seat.

"Bird?" Mom asks.

This time I chime in. "Mom, look out for the bir—"

Mom hits the break. There's an enormous black bird standing in the middle of the road.

"Is it . . . playing chicken?" says Delia, snorting at her own joke, and I hate myself for laughing a little, too, but this enormous black bird is just standing there in the middle of the road, looking straight at us through the windshield like it's daring us to move forward. I'm not sure how much more bizarre this trip can get.

"Just inch up," I suggest. "It'll move."

Yet even as I say the words aloud, something inside of me doubts I'm right. I can't stop staring at the bird—its onyx eyes, its tiny fluff of feathers hooding the top of its slightly hooked beak, its oil-slick feathers pushed tight against its large body. This bird has no intention of moving out of our way.

"Maybe just . . . move around it?" I say when I notice Mom realizing the same thing I am.

"Around it how?" Mom asks, and I see what she's saying. It's hard to know where the edge of the road stops and the forest starts. Who knows what lies underneath all that overgrowth? It could be a six-inch drop, or some furry animal's habitat. Or some creepy bird's ground nest full of hatchlings.

Mom eases the car in a slow semicircle around the bird, tires crunching over the forest bed.

"Why does that bird hate you?" Delia whispers from the back seat. No one answers. To be honest, I'm not really sure.

Once we're past it, Mom picks up a little speed, glancing one last time in her rearview mirror.

"It still hasn't moved," she says.

"I'm sure it was just protecting its nest," I posit.

"On the ground?" asks Delia unhelpfully.

As soon as we turn left, there stands another huge crow, stock-still in the middle of the road.

"You've got to be kidding," says Mom.

"Do you think . . . it's the same one?" says Delia, but if this is another of her jokes, none of us are laughing.

"It's not," I say, noticing immediately the distinct white feather sticking up from this one's head.

"This is nuts," says Mom, again edging around the crow in our path. "And not birdseed nuts." Again, the bird makes no move to fly away.

We're silent as we approach the next break in the trees, and when this sign points us to the right, we hold a collective breath and prepare for the crow that we're now sure will be waiting for us on the forest floor. Instead, the tree canopy thins, and what we see in place of the crow is a massive brick wall.

"What on earth?" Mom breathes.

I roll down the window and lean out to examine the wall, only to find it isn't actually a wall at all, but a sort of watchtower. I can see a turret at the top. Beside my head is a small metal box with a little black handle that says PULL.

Who am I to argue?

Inside the box is a tiny red button below a circular pattern of holes.

"I think it's a call box," I say, pushing the red button.

We're met with silence.

Mom leans over me toward the speaker anyway. "Hello? We're looking for Raven Brooks," she says. "Can you tell us if we're on the right track? We may have taken a wrong turn at the . . ."

"At the crow," Delia mutters. But that's absurd—there's no way that crow is a permanent fixture of the road.

Or is it? I think.

I scan the wall in front of me, looking for an actual door. Unless it's hidden in the mortar that joins the bricks somehow, I'm not seeing it.

What I am seeing, though, is the tiniest carving etched into the brick closest to the car tire on my side. I lean farther out of the window to get a better look, and what I see is . . . honestly, I'm not sure. What I am sure of is that I don't like it.

Someone has carved into the brick a sort of crude bird, except it doesn't look exactly like the birds that "greeted" us in the road. Instead, this looks like an unnatural cross between a man and a bird, standing on its two feet hunched and stooped, its neck sloped forward at an odd angle, its feathers hanging knotted and limp on long limbs that aren't quite arms but aren't quite wings, either. And unless my eyes are playing a trick on me, I'd swear that its beak is a set of teeny-tiny razors, ready to destroy whatever comes its way.

"I feel sick," Delia says behind me, and at first I think she's seeing the same carving in the brick that I am.

But when I turn, I see that she's pointing to a tattered piece of paper affixed to the brick farther down the wall. It says:

CLOSED FOR SEISMIC TESTING.

NO ENTRY.

"Huh?" Mom says. "How do you just close an entire town?"

"I wonder if this town was built on a fault line," I say.

"Maybe it's earthquake-prone." It's the only explanation I can think of. Though I'm not really sure crows are so attuned to seismic activity.

I take another look at the call box. Mom's given up on it.

"Should we give it another go?" I suggest.

Mom shakes her head. She's got another idea.

There's a ditch nearby with a culvert through it.

"I don't like it," Mom says. "But we could drive through that."

"Aw, come on. What's the worst that could happen?" Delia says. "So we drive through a little standing water in a giant ditch. Maybe we get a little radiation poisoning. Maybe we get some superpowers out of it."

Mom takes a deep breath. Then she hits the accelerator.

"Yes!" says Delia. "I hope I get turned into a centaur."

"You're not going to get turned into a—"

"A radioactive centaur!"

As we reach the mouth of the culvert, it's a little narrower than I thought. The top has a lower clearance, too. With a bunch of our luggage latched to the car roof, I'm a little nervous about it all clearing. I wouldn't care so much, except my sound equipment is in the box strapped to the very top of the car and some of it was a gift from Dad.

I hear my metal case scrape against the top of the tunnel and wince.

"You know what'd be great to see on the other side?" Delia says. "Another creepy bird. Ooo, maybe my first task as a radioactive centaur would be to fight it. Wouldn't that be fun to watch?"

I have no idea what we'll find on the other side of the ditch. A road? Another wall? A raccoon in a top hat? Another bird?

All I really want to find is home. My *new* home, I mean.

Mom is a master driver, and once she's successfully navigated us through, we indeed emerge on a road.

It couldn't all end that easily, though.

Seconds after Mom stops the car on the other side, the roof that fought so hard against my case full of sound equipment groans loud enough to make my ears hurt. With a sickening twist of metal, the brick wall that formed the top half of the culvert begins falling away in chunks. The tin roof of the tunnel bows at a tight angle toward the ground.

"Mom, it's going to—"

Mom is gripping the steering wheel hard enough that I think she might break it. She takes one trembling breath after another, but she can't seem to breathe slower.

Or maybe that's me.

Delia, however, is turned completely around in the back seat, hands gripping the headrest.

"That was amazing!" she screeches. "Do I have an extra eye?"

Mom's eye is starting to twitch. Must be the adrenaline—I feel it, too.

"Mom, you're like an action-movie hero!" says Delia.

Mom doesn't peel her eyes from the road. I shake my head.

What lies in front of us is more forest, dense and thick. But there's a road that runs alongside the tree line, and that's good enough. *It's something to follow*, Dad would have said, and thinking about him here with us gives me a twinge of hope.

"Huh," Mom says, looking at the dashboard. "The outside thermometer must be off. It says it's sixty-five degrees."

Sixty-five degrees? In the middle of summer? That seems unlikely, but Mom's right—I'd instinctively turned the air conditioner off right when we pulled through the ditch.

Delia rolls down her window, and immediately, a brisk wind rushes through the car. But there's more than that. The smell is different, too. It smells like fall.

I peer closer at the trees alongside the road, and while most of them are some form or another of evergreen, there are some leaf-shedding ones, too. And those leaves are the telltale colors of autumn, their varied shades looking like leaves on fire.

Mom commands Delia to roll up the window as we all brush away a chill.

"Just checking, that wasn't a time portal, right?" I ask.

Mom keeps driving. "It's just an unseasonably cool day," she says. "Must have something to do with all the branches. Well, that's fine by me. You know I hate the heat anyway."

But if we thought the weirdness was going to subside once we actually drove into town, we were so far off.

Driving into town is like seeing two different worlds—a thicket of wilderness on our right, and a fully developed town on our left. The houses that line the street along the left all face the forest, as though to watch it. Their yards are alternately littered with toys or adorned with crumbling birdbaths, well-weeded or carelessly groomed. There are two-story, skinny houses and flat

ranch-styles, small boxy ones and wide, shambling ones. They all look lived-in, though not currently inhabited. It's like we've missed the memo about a meeting or something.

"It is the middle of the day," Mom says, reading my mind. "I'm sure everyone is just at work or school."

But it's a Saturday in July. I seriously doubt that.

Mom drives until she reaches a traffic light, red for absolutely no reason. It's not like there's anyone crossing, but rules are rules, so we wait.

I stare at a billboard that's towering above us. It's faded and shredding, but a billboard nonetheless.

It's got a picture of a bunch of kids, all dressed in retro nineties garb. There's a boy with a head full of messy dark hair and a wobbly smile and another with light brown hair. I can't understand why, but he has a sad face. It's like none of his features can pretend enough to make him look happy. Then there's a freckled girl holding a little rag doll, and another girl with her chin cupped in her hand, a dimple so sweet she looks like the stock photo that comes with a new picture frame. Then, all the way to the left of the row, is an image that looks like it might have been added later, judging by the more modern clothes and crispness of the image. He's the only adult, and his salt-and-pepper goatee and wire-rimmed glasses make him look equal parts smart and kind. I can't help but think he was added in later, almost like he were *just* pasted in a second ago. It's strange seeing them all together, looming overhead in this suburban forest town.

Then I see the text above their images:

NO MORE MISSING. NO MORE LOST.

"This is the longest traffic light in history," Delia says, and she's saying what I'm feeling, because all I want to do is be away from that billboard and this creepy spot.

Suddenly, a low rumble breaks our uncomfortable silence. I'd think it was thunder if there were even one cloud in the sky.

The voices are still too far away to make out, but there are enough of them to make a cloud of noise loud enough to ripple the air.

"Mom?" Delia says from the back, leaning forward between our two seats.

"I hear it, too," she replies. It's a mob. An angry mob?

"I think it's coming from over there," I say, pointing ahead to an area tucked into one of the residential streets.

"They sound . . ." Delia starts tentatively.

"Mad," I finish.

All of a sudden, the front door to a pink house directly to our left opens.

Out flies a woman my mom's age, with thick dark hair pulled into a messy ponytail. She has kind eyes, and a wave of calm washes over me . . . until I notice she's running toward our car.

CHAPTER 2

There's exactly no time for any of us to react.

"Quick, before they see you!" the woman yells. "Into my garage. Come quick!"

Mom does something I've never seen her do. She freezes.

"Mom," I say, making the decision. After all, it's this lady or the mob. "Let's do it."

She looks like she's about to argue. Honestly, she probably should. I have no idea why I think it's a good idea to listen to this frantic stranger and hide in her garage. But there's something about her that looks familiar. I can't place it. Almost like I'd just seen her.

"Come *on*!" the woman says, backing away and pointing to her open garage.

"Do it, Mom!" Delia says, catching the urgency like it's contagious. "Do it to activate my radioactive centaur powers!"

I guess "radioactive centaur powers" is the magic phrase, because Mom cuts the wheel hard and zooms into the woman's driveway. Her garage door closes and cloaks us in pitch dark.

We sit there for a moment in stunned silence.

Then, just as I'm about to ask what we should do next, the

door leading to the house cracks open, and the woman pops her head through.

"I'm so sorry," the woman says, and it sounds like she means it. "This must not make any sense to you. I'll come back when it's safe. Just . . . don't leave. Whatever you do, stay here. Stay put. I have some water and granola bars in the garage. Help yourself."

She's so stern, I don't dare argue. It looks like Mom might, but the woman closes the door and once again, we're left in stunned silence.

I open my door a crack. The woman's garage smells identical to ours from home—*our old home*, I have to get used to saying. Maybe it's the strange chemistry of garage odors—cardboard boxes and gasoline vapors, dried leaves and paint supplies. Whatever it is, suddenly I'm back in our house, and we're arriving home from some recital or boring family road trip. Delia and I are racing out of the car to be the first to light the Hanukkah lights. Mom is loading us up with grocery bags. Dad is reaching for the box of old candles.

Dad is alive.

I'm eight years old, and he's alive. I'm eleven years old. I'm seven. I'm five.

And Dad is alive.

"It sounds like the voices outside are getting closer," I hear Delia say, and she's right. The rumble has all but disappeared under the clear sound of shouts. And though they are loud, their shouts are still indecipherable from one another.

Mom nods. "You two stay right here." She peels out of the car and presses her ear to the garage door.

Of course, we don't listen, and follow her to the garage door that separates us from the flood of people headed in our direction.

Mom peers through one of the cracks along the side of the closed door, and Delia and I peek through the other side.

Finally, I see the first members of the mob trickle into view. I stupidly expect them to be carrying torches and pitchforks, but instead, they're armed with flashlights, which I have to admit is a strange choice to be carrying in the middle of the day.

"They're coming right toward us," Delia whispers.

I squint at the approaching crowd, hoping she's wrong, but it definitely looks like they're headed this way.

"Shh," Mom commands.

We all watch in horrified silence as the mob fills the street outside, a never-ending deluge of angry, shouting people waving fists and flashlights.

They're close enough now that I think I can make out what at least one voice is saying, not that it makes any sense.

"This ends today!"

Another voice contributes to the din. "We're not leaving until we find him!" shouts another.

Him?

Are they talking about one of the people pictured on the billboard?

I'm just trying to wrap my brain around it when I see the very same woman with the messy ponytail and wide brown eyes traveling among the crowd, flashlight in each hand.

Which could mean nothing at all.

Except they're headed right for us. And she knows we're in her garage.

But there's no way this can be about us . . .

Right?

Then, just as she takes a step in our direction, the woman with the wide brown eyes guides the crowd away and chants.

"No more lost! No more lost!"

I hear Mom let out a breath I didn't know she was holding. When I look down at Delia, I realize she's not staring through the crack in the garage door anymore. She's staring up at me.

It's okay, I mouth to her, and she gives me the tiniest nod.

"No more lost! No more lost!"

Now the crowd heads toward the woods. They stop along the forest's edge, and I see someone raise their hand at the front. The crowd falls silent.

"Remember, groups of five, and absolutely *no one* leaves their team. If you hear anything, if you see anything, if you *smell* anything, blow your whistle."

The crowd is so silent, I can hear Delia struggling to breathe quietly below me.

The man at the front scans the crowd, then says, "Now let's go find him."

The mass of people breaks into clusters of five and filters through the dense tree line and into the forest, disappearing from sight almost the second they pass the first tree. The last person to enter the forest is the woman with the large brown eyes. She pauses for no more than a second, glances back in our direction, and then turns to follow the crowd.

Only now do I realize that they've entered the forest in almost the exact spot where the billboard rises above the tree line.

I'm trembling.

"Okay," Mom says after a while. "Get in the car."

Delia grabs a granola bar from the box that the woman pointed to, and we both climb back in. But Mom doesn't. Instead, she walks to the wall by the door that leads to what I can only assume is the woman's house. Before I can ask, Mom hits the button to open the automatic garage door, then climbs back into the driver's seat.

"What are you doing?" I blurt. "They could be back any second!"

"Which is why we're leaving right now."

"But the lady—"

"Is a stranger," Mom says, reversing down the driveway in a hurry. "I have zero intentions of following orders from someone who effectively trapped us in her garage. I don't know why I listened in the first place. This whole thing is absurd."

"She has good taste in granola bars," Delia pipes up from the back, crumbs scattering everywhere.

"Who? The lady? The people with flashlights? The birds?" The pitch of Mom's voice is rising with each guess. She's got this wild look in her eyes, and I don't think it's from the many hours on the road.

"Where are we going?" I ask, because as far as I can tell,

Mom isn't making headway toward the address that the real estate agent gave us.

"As far away from Raven Brooks as I can get us," Mom says, and for the first time since turning down that brush-covered road off the two-lane highway, I feel slightly more at ease. We're not staying.

Whatever this town is, it isn't for us. It's like at every turn, something has tried to keep us out. We can take a hint.

"We can't go back the way we came," says Delia, not exactly impressed with our action-movie entrance anymore.

Mom considers this. "That cannot be the only way out of this town," she says.

We go searching for an exit. Mom decides the best course of action is to drive until we find an edge of town, then follow the edge until we find a way out. Seems like a decent strategy, except that the first time we hit a dead end down a residential street, it's actually a cul-de-sac. No option to make a right or a left.

"That's okay," Mom says, not yet defeated. "We'll look for a commercial road instead. One of those has to connect to an interstate or something."

But when we drive down Main Street—the actual definition of a commercial road, with its empty and shuttered shops (pre-sumably because everyone has taken to the forest, because that's completely normal on a Saturday afternoon)—we hit yet another dead end in the form of—wait for it—the forest.

"These trees!" Mom screeches, exasperated. "How does anyone get around here?"

"Let's try the other direction," I suggest, and Mom U-turns and takes us down the other side of the empty road.

We drive slowly enough to take in a little bit more of the town that would have been our home if it hadn't greeted us with a truckload of weirdness.

It all looks so . . . normal. The shops on Main Street are precisely what I would expect shops on someplace called "Main Street" to be. There's a cupcake place, at least three coffee shops, a sushi restaurant, a couple of taquerias. There's a hardware store and a handful of colorful bodega-type shops with some normal-looking signs that say things like "We cash checks," "NEW vegan flavors here," and "We have ice." Honestly, it's exactly the kind of place I wouldn't have minded exploring a little more, if it weren't for the utter, and I mean *utter,* weirdness.

As we follow the bend in the road, Main Street turns into an unnamed street that once again borders the forest that seems to be the primary resident in Raven Brooks.

"I'm sure this will lead to a way out," Delia says.

The empty asphalt dips and bends, and every few seconds, I cast a wary glance at the wall of trees to our left, half expecting the giant herd of townspeople to emerge from the thicket and congregate ahead, blocking our path.

Instead, once we top another dip and hill, we see a different kind of roadblock.

Mom lowers her head to the steering wheel.

"Another brick wall?" asks Delia.

I shake my head.

25

"The same brick wall."

One continuous wall. Where there isn't a wall, there are trees. Where there aren't trees, there's a wall.

The entirety of Raven Brooks is a town in a bubble.

"It might not be the same—"

"It's the same," I say, trying not to sound defeated while there's still a tiny flame of hope burning in Delia. "We went in a circle."

"Around the entire town," says Mom, her head still buried in the steering wheel.

I take out my phone, but it's no use. If we couldn't get a signal on the other side of those trees, we certainly can't get one in here.

I search for any nearby Wi-Fi to piggyback on, but the only network that appears as an option is RB1-Public. And the *last* thing I want to do is share my cell phone data with Raven Brooks, RB, whatever.

I shake my head in wonder. "They have their own network."

My stomach grumbles, and when I look at the dash, the clock says 7:45. It's late. Maybe Delia was right to grab that granola bar after all.

Mom looks at Delia and me. It's a look she has a lot these days, like she's assessing the weight of our entire world in a matter of seconds. Then I see her face light up, like she's got an idea.

"We're going to Cousin Marcia's," Mom says finally.

Cousin Marcia's. The original plan.

"We're . . . staying," I say, though I'm not sure if it's a question or a statement.

But the answer is all over Mom's face. What choice do we have? It's either that or sleep in the car tonight. Either way, it doesn't look like we're getting out of Raven Brooks until morning.

"We have a key to an apartment," Mom says. "And let's be honest. We need the rest."

I sigh. My phone may not be connected to any form of network, but it still has the address and original directions saved. We continue on.

CHAPTER 3

Mom referred to Cousin Marcia like someone we'd known forever. But to be honest, Delia and I only heard about her for the first time last month.

Marcia Tillman was a cousin of my dad's, so technically she's probably our great-cousin or whatever. She and Dad died only a few days apart, her first, and for some reason or another, she gifted us her apartment and her indie grocery store in her will. I don't think I remember Dad ever talking about Marcia, either, which made it all the weirder. But it all seemed very serendipitous. Exactly three days after my dad's funeral, here was this official-looking letter from a lawyer we'd never heard of from a town we'd never heard of on behalf of a cousin of Dad's we'd never met. It had seemed, at the time, like Dad was giving us some kind of path forward . . . especially because his business partner pointed the finger at my father for the entire legal mess their company was in, and he was dead, so he couldn't really defend himself. Mom was pretty eager to get us out, I protested, the hair dye happened, and then the rest was history.

But now, stuck in the car, it feels like a long time ago that Cousin Marcia and her "Natural Grocer" felt like something that could make us whole again.

We're quiet again, except for me giving my mom turn-by-turn directions. The streets are fully dark now, and not a single streetlamp lights our way, but Mom is hesitant to turn on the headlights. We still haven't seen a single person since watching the town disappear into the forest, and our only goal now is to get to the Natural Grocer unnoticed. From there, we can eat. We can rest. And in the morning, we can figure out how to leave, ruffling as few feathers as possible on our way out.

At last, we approach a small, boarded-up shop roughly the size of a one-story house. A dirty, unlit sign reads NATURAL GROCER, with the *G* formed by what appears to be a squirrel tail and the store name resting atop a bed of leaves. Above the shop sits an apartment that looks to have been placed there by a giant claw. If it's attached to the store in any way, it looks like it's held on by a few nails and some wood glue. I can't help but think maybe it's for the best this isn't our new home.

We drive around to the back of the store and pull the car into one of the two empty spaces set aside for the Natural Grocer. If the apartment looks unstable in its placement, the stairs leading up to the front door look like they're one breath away from total collapse.

"You first," Delia says to me, burying her elbow in my rib.

"Nope," I reply. "Spares before heirs."

It's an old joke that's grown less funny over the months now that Dad is gone.

It's Mom who pushes ahead, fishing the keys out of the folder pocket that the real estate agent had mailed to us.

Mom tried to do research on Raven Brooks before moving,

but there was nothing to be found. The real-estate-agent-slash-estate-lawyer said it was a quaint and quiet place, and after everything that happened with Dad's business partner, it seemed like exactly what we needed. Mom had complained about broken links and websites under construction from her cursory searches. From what I knew, there were only obscure mentions of the town here and there but no record of its existence on any state or federal database. And for us, wanting to start a new life, it seemed almost magical.

Pah. I could laugh.

The rest of the binder held some semi-indecipherable paperwork from the lawyer; a deed for the store and another for the apartment; inexplicably, Cousin Marcia's Raven Brooks Library card with a small Post-it stuck to it reading *USE ME!*; and a set of keys with a clunky but kinda cool key ring attached to it. Delia and I had both wanted it—a ruby-red chip set in a sort of circular steampunk-looking dial with a moveable wheel. It was heavy, too. It made a loud *thunk!* when Mom would swing the ring around her finger while she was searching for nonexistent information on Raven Brooks. She decided that since we both argued over it, it was hers. I guess when you're the parent that's what you get to decide.

Now Mom strides ahead of us, swinging the key ring on her finger and fidgeting with the dial. We're each carrying a suitcase, some clothes for a few days and a toothbrush. The rest of our stuff is with the movers. After all, we couldn't fit *all* that much in our car.

Mom takes the first tentative step on the stairs, and they groan as she passes. She pauses, rigid, before taking another step. Again, the staircase groans.

"Better let me open the door first," Mom narrates. We'll take the steps one person at a time.

When Mom unlocks the door and pushes in, Delia goes next, taking the first few steps carefully before practically sprinting to the top and disappearing through the door.

I'm just about to take my first step when the unmistakable smell of smoke fills my nostrils.

I lift my nose, turning in place to try to get a better sense of where the smell is coming from, but it's impossible to tell, even on the chilly, still night air. I can't see any sign of flame or smoke no matter where I look.

What I *do* know is that wherever the smell is coming from, it's close. And for reasons I can't explain, it feels like I'm being watched.

I'm not careful on the stairs. I don't even take a test step. I thunder up like a kid fleeing a dark basement.

I'm at the top of the steps before I know it, and I swing the door shut fast enough to make my mom and my sister jump.

I twist the bolt and lock the handle. "Just in case," I say, feeling stupid but not stupid enough to leave the door unlocked.

Mom nods. She gets it. She doesn't turn on the light. She doesn't want to draw any attention to the apartment in case someone drives by. Instead, we rely on the light from the moon streaming in through the windows, and the flashlights on our phones, though we have to preserve those batteries. Weirdly, I can't find an outlet in sight.

Even as the shades of gray cast throughout the shadows of the tiny residence, the place looks shabby. And not homey-shabby. It looks like Cousin Marcia barely cared about the place. Corners of furniture, all mismatched and well-worn, are chipped and splintered. The sofa is threadbare, covered in an equally threadbare woolen orange blanket. There's a small, sad kitchen off to the right, and a little alcove beside it that creates a half-moon breakfast bar.

A two-bedroom apartment with one bathroom to share between us, a kitchen with a two-burner stove, and exotic bird wallpaper was to be our new address. 57½ Old Farm Road, Raven Brooks: an address so small, it only gets half a number.

"I . . . uh . . . I think your room is straight ahead," Mom says, and I can tell she's doing her best to sound optimistic, but no matter how she talks, I can hear the deepening disappointment in her voice. "You know, your room for the night." She says "night" as if to emphasize "we are leaving first thing in the morning." None of this is going the way it was supposed to.

Delia and I shuffle the short distance from the front door to the small bedroom, wooden floors creaking under the faded rugs scattered here and there. I break into a sudden sprint to reach the tiny bedroom, determined to claim the best bed. As it turns out, they're identical, but I still find a reason to count mine as the best.

"I get the window seat," I say.

"I get the bed closest to the door," she says, and I don't follow until she adds, "Closest to the exit."

I nod. "How survivalist of you."

"I have good instincts," she says.

"You have slow legs. Otherwise you'd have the window seat."

Mom locates her room on the other side of the closet-sized bathroom, and Delia and I retrieve our bags from the living room, the only ones we bothered taking out of the car.

As I crack mine open, it's like a time capsule of what I thought would be important to have on this first night in Raven Brooks. Crazy how it feels like a lifetime ago that I had the audacity to believe that arriving in our new home would feel normal.

I take inventory of what I thought I'd need:

- My softest nightshirt and a change of underwear
- Socks in case the floors were cold (they are)
- Every device charger known to humankind, even though, again, there's no outlets
- A super-sized tub of pita chips
- A brand-new toothbrush and my favorite kind of toothpaste that tastes like salty baking soda
- Color-safe shampoo
- Mr. and Mr. Badger (Stuffed animals in suits—one blue and one green—that Dad brought back for us after a business trip to Napa. Delia and I decided they made the perfect couple, and since they were already in formal wear, it made sense that they would be married.)

I toss one of the Mr. Badgers to Delia, and she gives him a quick snuggle before laying him on her pillow. We change into our pajamas and meet Mom back in the living room. I'm holding the pita chips, and Delia is holding a bag of apples.

"Five dollars to the first person who finds the thermostat," Mom says, and we feel along the walls until my hand runs over a small box near the kitchen.

Even with the heat rattling away in the baseboards lining the walls, the chill in the air is relentless.

Shivering, we drag our blankets from our beds and crowd around the coffee table, making dinner from apples and pita chips, wondering how it came to this.

"It'll be better in the morning," Mom says, but I don't even know if she believes it.

"First thing tomorrow, we'll pack up and find our way out."

Delia says it first. Maybe because she's braver. What's that saying? Always trust the youth? "Then where will we go?"

Maybe Mom doesn't hear her. The pita chips are a little stale, so their crunch is loud.

But no, I think she hears her. She just doesn't have an answer.

After we give up on dinner, Delia and Mom manage to fall asleep. All I can do is lie on my bed by the window and stare at the ceiling, my memory creating a slideshow of the day's bizarre events.

The birds, the culvert, the lady and her garage. The endless sea of trees and the billboard of missing people. The brick wall fencing us in, refusing to let us out. The burning that filled my nose as I stood outside alone.

Then, as though I conjure it with just my memory, the smell wafts back to me. It's fainter this time. But it's definitely here again.

I sit up fast, my vision going black for a second before I can refocus on the dark of the room.

From the corner of my eye, something in the window looms.

I turn slowly, searching the lightless street below for what must be there. It doesn't take me long to find it.

Lingering in the shadow cast by a nearby building is a hulking figure.

My breath catches at the sight of it, but I can't seem to look away. I can make out a loose form—road, hunched shoulders, long limbs . . . and what must be a head but some trick of shadow is making it look pointed.

Like a beak.

An image of the bird in the road looms in my head, and as my pulse quickens, I squint and try to make sense of what I'm seeing. When that doesn't work, I rub my eyes and wait for the spots of light to clear, my heart pounding harder with each passing second.

It's just a shadow. It's just a shadow.

When I take my hands away, the shadow has changed to something even harder to define. It looks more man than bird now, its pointed beak more of a curled handlebar against its face, too big to be a mustache, glowing at its sides like it's set against a fire.

I squeeze my eyes shut again, opening this time to a flash of white.

But when my vision finally returns, it isn't anything. The shadow is gone.

I press my forehead to the glass and look up and down the night-soaked street, but all I see is asphalt. Even the smell of burning is gone.

I lie back down and stare at the ceiling, more certain than before that I will not be sleeping tonight. Every time I try closing my eyes, I see that shadow, looming close enough for me to smell it.

Every time I open my eyes again, I tell myself that it's not possible the shadow was looking right at me.

CHAPTER 4

nce upon a time, Sundays could be counted on for sleeping in. Shades would stay drawn, feet would tiptoe, and sometimes, even the sun would agree to rise just a little later.

But Cousin Marcia never bothered to put a shade on this window, and Delia's feet don't know how to tiptoe, and nothing is the way it's supposed to be anymore.

"Get dressed!" Delia shrieks in my ear.

All of yesterday and the night before wash over me in a wave. I accidentally let out a snort.

Delia jumps back. "OMG, you're like a giant boar!"

"You scared me!"

"I've never heard you make that sound."

"Maybe I've never been scared that badly!"

"Maybe you're half boar. Half *radioactive* boar!"

"Girls!"

Delia remembers why she woke me up.

"C'mon," she says, tugging on my arm.

"Are we leaving already?" I ask. I'm eager to go, too, but I also like my beauty sleep.

Delia's eyes widen. She clenches her teeth to make her voice quieter. Somehow, it works.

"We aren't leaving *at all*."

That's enough to get me out of bed.

Mom's sitting at the kitchen table.

"So," she begins. "I've been thinking."

If by "thinking," Mom means she stayed up all night teasing her hair and drawing dark circles under her eyes, then she's been thinking *hard*.

"Why on earth would we let a few birds and some protesters chase us away from our new home?" she asks. "Wildlife is wild-life anywhere. Protests are good. It shows people are actively participating in social issues. Heck, maybe we should find out what they were about and join, too."

Her eyes are wide. Like, fishing-for-her-contacts wide.

"It was the end of a very long day. A long *few* days, really," she continues. "In the light of a new day, I think it's pretty obvi-ous that we were all overreacting a little."

I must not be hearing her right. My ears are still waking up.

"But the wall," Delia says, her voice quieter than usual.

Mom shrugs. "Probably just a retaining wall. Plenty of towns have them, for rain and whatnot," she says. "Just because we didn't find a way in or out doesn't mean there isn't one. I mean, we also didn't ask."

"Mom, I really think we had the right idea last night," I say, trying to appeal to whatever rational part of Mom is left in this sleepless shell standing before us.

"I bet after a good breakfast and a little time out in the sun, we'll feel differently," Mom says.

This version of Mom isn't one I think I've ever seen. The

Mom I'm used to I wouldn't describe her as perky. I wouldn't even say she's optimistic. She's more of a . . . pragmatic worrier.

"What sun?" says Delia, motioning toward the window. She's right; it's a gloomy day. The sun doesn't have a chance against all those clouds.

"Okay, well, there's still UV rays on cloudy days, which means we'll wear sunscreen. And there's fresh air. Maybe we'll go for a walk, explore our new neighborhood," says Mom.

"Mom, let's talk rationally," I say. "You really want . . . this . . . to be your new neighborhood? You want to walk outside to that woman from last night and say, 'Hello, neighbor!'?"

Mom's brow furrows but only for a second.

"Piper," she says, this time a full octave lower. "We have nowhere else to go."

She sinks into the squeaky couch, dropping her head into her hands and hiding her face. After a second, I hear her sniffle.

My heart sinks. We made her cry.

Delia and I sit on either side of Mom and take turns apologizing.

"It's not your fault," Mom says, wiping her eyes roughly. "None of it is your fault."

"We can stay if you want," Delia says.

Mom laughs, but there's zero humor in it. "I don't want to," she admits. "But what choice do we have? We have nowhere else to go, and the court is still settling your father's insurance claims. It was quite fortunate that Cousin Marcia left us all . . . well, all of this."

She drops her head again.

Mom shakes her head despairingly. The tears are falling freely now. It doesn't matter how many times I see Mom cry. It always makes me want to run and hide. I haven't yet, though. Not once.

"Dwight took everything. He took it all," Mom continues.

Dwight. Dad's business partner. The one who pinned every wrong thing on my dad after he was gone. After he couldn't defend himself with the truth. Apparently, Dwight wasn't done hurting us.

"You mean he—" I start.

"Everything your father worked so hard for," Mom says, her throat thickening. She's getting ready to cry again. "There wouldn't even be a business to steal if your dad hadn't . . . and now Dwight . . ."

The tears are back. And I'm back to wishing I could hide.

Mom collects herself again. That doesn't mean I like what she has to say, though.

"The shop is all we have."

Her words drop like anvils.

"*Raven Brooks* is all we have."

And there it is. Every reason in the world to stay. We could hop in the car right now, our clothes and toothbrushes and pita chips repacked and tucked under our feet. We could drive and drive and drive until we find the exit to this bizarre little town full of shadows and phantom fires.

But even if we found the way out, we couldn't leave.

"So . . ." Mom says, staring blankly ahead of her as though the words might appear before her on the wall.

"So . . ." Delia says.

"So . . ." I say, and someone has to find the words. I guess it might as well be me. "So, let's go check out the store."

* * *

I might be the first person in the world to hear the actual sound of a heart dropping. Three hearts, actually.

"It's . . . quaint."

"It . . . has potential."

Mom drops the key with its giant silver disk key ring. It hits the polished concrete floor, right where I imagine her heart landed.

"It's a dump."

The Natural Grocer is, in fact, a dump. There really isn't any denying that fact, and none of us has the energy to muster any more lies. The place should have been condemned a year ago, maybe sooner. It smells vaguely of rotting produce, even though any perishables have long since been cleared out. The refrigerator case lining the back wall is empty and dark, its doors open, presumably to keep the must out, not that it's helped much.

Mom crosses the store to try switching on the refrigeration, but she's met with a sputtering sound, a flicker of lights, and with a giant pop, one of the bulbs inside the case shatters, causing the whole case to go dark again.

"Of course." Mom sighs.

The aisles that zigzag before us are still stocked with boxes and cans and packages of items boasting a longer shelf life—everything from dried lentils to probiotic capsules to gluten-free waffle mix. A cash register lies under a vinyl cover like a sleeping bird in its cage.

"Mom, if anyone can make this into something, it's you," says Delia.

That's the truth, and if anyone needs a good helping of truth telling, I recommend asking Delia. Two years younger than me and already outshining nearly every effort I make at being a decent person, this girl is my hero. But I solemnly swear to never *ever* tell her that.

"Piper, I'm putting you on coffee duty," Mom says. "If you can find an unexpired can or bag of anything resembling caffeine, I'll buy whatever hair dye you want."

"Can I get in on that?" Delia pipes up. "Rainbow might look cool."

Mom manages a nod, and Delia and I set to the task, scouring the dusty shelves for beans or grounds. Delia locates the aisle of teas and supplements first, but I'm a step ahead as usual. Apparently, the week the Natural Grocer had finally gone under, Cousin Marcia had been clearing out old stock. A display piled high with Jumpin' Jake's Coffee Flakes lurks in the far corner of the store, nearest to what was once the produce section.

I blow the dust from the top of the closest box and slide it into Mom's hand.

"You're my favorite for the day," she says.

Delia scrambles around the corner, fanning three bars of organic cacao bars like a winning poker hand.

"Before you decide," she says to Mom, "I brought chocolate."

I stare Delia down. "Well played, but the deal was coffee."

We look to Mom, the final judge, and she gives up in record time.

"You each get anything you want in the store."

"Hey!" I say. It's technically *our* store, but I'm not bartering with Mom.

Delia and I crack open the chocolate bars, which appear to need a jackhammer to break the bricks apart. I pop one of the squares into my mouth, and I have never regretted anything faster.

Delia pushes her brick to the side of her mouth, wincing against the taste. "Maybe if you just, you know, savor it for a minute."

"It tastes like cow poop," I say, forcing back the nausea. "This isn't chocolate. This isn't even mocklate. This is . . . this is a betrayal," I say, and I swear my eyes start to water. It might be sadness. It might be that my taste buds are being tortured. Who would ever make chocolate taste this . . . bad?

Mom doesn't even bother with niceties. The square was in her mouth for maybe three-fifths of a second before it rocketed back out, landing with a clink on the floor. An *actual* clink.

She eyes the can of Jumpin' Jake's Coffee Flakes. "Maybe there's a place in town we can pick up some supplies today."

Delia's eyes flash. "You mean, like, check out the competition?" Delia loves a mission.

"She means we're going to get groceries," I mutter.

"We're going to scope out the competition," she says, retrieving her keys with the ruby key chain from the floor and dropping them in her purse.

Mom sashays through the front door and leaves us to follow.

I look at Delia. "We're going to get groceries."

* * *

We end up at another grocery store called the Food Barn. The Food Barn is living up to every bit of its kitschy name. The entire warehouse-sized store is barn-themed: bales of hay and cornhusk displays, signage that looks like it's been carved by some old dude rocking on a porch wielding a pocketknife.

"This place is massive!" Delia cries the second we walk through the automatic doors.

Every head in the store turns in our direction, and at first I think it's because Delia is loud. Then I think it's because our hair is perhaps a shade or two bolder than anyone else's in the store; Delia is rocking teal these days.

I look at Mom for answers, because even after the obligatory second or two of solid staring, people aren't looking away in embarrassment. Common courtesy would have them sneaking glances when they think we aren't looking. But no, this is bold staring. This is *aggressive* staring.

We are officially aquarium fish.

Maybe if we try a little harder to blend, it'll be less obvious that we are NEW WITH BIG BOLD FLASHING LIGHTS.

"Uh," I stammer, pulling on Mom's sleeve to get her to move it along. "Let's see if there's falafel," naming Mom's favorite food.

Before I know it, we're walking beside her as she pushes a cart with purpose through the brightly lit store. Delia and I are taking turns sliding contraband into the cart, getting closer to catching Mom's attention with each furtive drop of Cocoa Puffs and salt-and-vinegar crackers.

But Mom is singularly focused on the prepackaged display at the back of the store—the one that might have her falafel. Well, that and the painfully obvious slacked jaws we pass in every single aisle, each shopper more baffled by us than the last.

"Okay, seriously, they *sell* purple hair dye here. How can we be such a spectacle?" I say, not bothering to lower my voice. It's getting old.

"Do I have boogers?" Delia says, flaring her nostrils and pitching her head skyward for me to look.

"All clear," I say.

"Then it must be my radioactivity," she says, and I can only shrug because how many oddities can you try to make sense of in less than two days? My brain is starting to hurt.

As usual, though, I can't seem to keep my superhuman

observation in check, so while Mom is searching the case for a manufacturer's label or maintenance phone number and Delia is sneaking pudding packs into the cart, I'm scoping everyone out who's scoping us out.

Maybe it's because I haven't been able to get warm all morning, but the first thing I notice is that everyone in the store seems to be clued into the same unseasonal weather. It's like the entire town got the memo that July in Raven Brooks is actually November, and they've dug out their puffy vests and all-weather boots four months too early.

Maybe it isn't the purple hair. Maybe it's our T-shirts and shorts that has us sticking out like sore thumbs. But how can I help it? It's all I packed in that one overnight suitcase, and our winter stuff is all with the movers, waiting to be shipped to us.

"Hey, I'm going to see if I can find any almond milk," I say, but Mom is barely listening. I leave her and Delia to the packaged foods and try to understand the other shoppers in the store.

I pad down the aisles, when I hear a voice.

"Tillman?" it says.

I jump back and catch myself right before knocking over a tower of boxed pumpkin bread mix. A girl small enough to be Delia's age but definitely older emerges from behind the pile. It's her hair I notice first because it's amazing. Shiny dark and bone-straight, even from the front, I can see it reaches all the way down to the middle of her back, but the sides are pulled away from her face in a series of intricate braids interwoven with the surrounding hair. It's like a labyrinth of strands coiling in and out and under until the ends disappear underneath the part that falls down her back. Matching silver braided rings adorn most of her fingers, and she has huge, familiar brown eyes that grow wider when she watches me practically eat it right there on the Food Barn floor.

"Huh?" I say. Which pretty much sums up how great I am at meeting new people.

"Tillman," she says, her eyes still wide, and now they're doing this dancing thing, like she wants to smile but she's holding out for now. "You must be related to Marcia Tillman. You have her hands. They're very pretty."

I have Cousin Marcia's . . . what?

Now the girl smiles. This town has me so messed up. I can't tell if she's making fun of me or trying to be my friend.

"Er—yeah. I'm Piper Tillman," I reply.

"Jess," she says, holding her hand up in a half wave.

"You must be new," Jess says, her smile fading a little. "We don't get a lot of new people."

"You don't say."

Jess's smile all but disappears. "You probably shouldn't be here."

I have no idea how to take this. Is she teasing me? Sarcasm is a funny thing. It works until it doesn't.

But just as Jess is turning around to leave me in the land of Eternal Fall, she stoops to a shelf I can't see from where I'm standing and rises, holding a folded sweater.

"Size large?"

"Thanks," I say, wishing I could put it on right now. "Is it always so cold here?"

Jess's face freezes in this weird, contorted smile, and I think for a second maybe her mouth got stuck, but she shakes it off quickly before answering, "Lately? Yeah. That's why there are sweaters in the grocery store. Anyway, we'll swing by later."

She walks away before I have a chance to process what she just said.

Who's "we"?

I'm still puzzling over it when I grab two more hoodies for Mom and Delia. When I return to the deli case, I see that Mom and my sister have attracted some attention. Well, *more* attention.

"I really didn't mean to pry," I hear Mom saying to a guy who has apparently migrated over from behind the deli counter. The olive-sample woman and the kimchi-display guy are here, too, and suddenly, it looks as though Mom is facing a grocery inquisition. Like a strange sort of food mafia has converged on her in the five minutes I was away.

"Then what exactly *were* you looking for in my case?" says a man in a white apron and plastic hairnet.

"He's *really* protective of his food case," Delia whispers to me, filling me in on the drama.

"Just a phone number!" Mom says defensively. I'm getting the impression this line of questioning has been going on for a little while.

"Who did you say you were again?" says the man from the kimchi counter. He's wearing a plastic cover over his ample beard and eyeing my mom closely.

"I don't think I caught your name, either," she says. I believe she would call that "sass" if I did it.

The kimchi-counter guy crosses his burly arms over his apron. "Carl. Carl Gaston. And everyone in town knows me. I'm pretty sure we can't say the same about you."

Mom crosses her arms over her T-shirt. "And at this rate, nobody's going to get to know us," she says.

"Who exactly signed you in? I don't remember Marcia mentioning any cousin she'd be turning the store over to," says the olive-sample lady. She's still holding her tray. I can see a few shoppers cruising by slowly. I think they came for the olives but stayed for the drama.

Okay, so they know we're related to Cousin Marcia. That much is clear.

"Signed us in? What do you—"

"The poor woman's only just passed," says the kimchi guy, shaking his head in disgust, and honestly, I'd expect more from a fellow spicy-fermented-food lover.

Mom's about to scream, and I don't blame her at all. I'm this close to poking kimchi-counter guy in the eye with one of the olive toothpicks. But Delia looks scared, and this isn't what we came for. We came for food, and maybe some information, and if we leave here with just food, maybe we can still salvage the trip.

"Cousin," I say, slapping on my most innocent face. "On our dad's side. He died."

I don't do this. I never do this. I don't use Dad's memory for getting out of sticky situations. But desperate times call for desperate measures.

"Oh," says kimchi-counter guy, an unlikely first person to soften.

"I guess tragedy isn't too hard to come by these days," says the olive lady, then, absurdly, offers up her tray.

I take an olive, though. I mean, I *am* hungry. Delia takes one, too. Mom isn't ready yet, though. I'm not, either, but what I *am* ready for is to leave this store.

"I, uh, I can get you the name of my maintenance guy," the kimchi man says, shoving his hands into the pockets of his khakis before retreating to the refrigerated back room.

"What . . . what just happened here?" Mom says, and now I hear what she wouldn't let any of the store employees hear. She's hurt.

"Not everyone is rude," I say, remembering Jess with the braids and how she, uh, complimented my hands? "Maybe they all just really liked Cousin Marcia."

"Yeah," Delia says, entertaining that theory. "They're just being good friends to her. Or, you know, her memory. It's not like *we* knew her, either."

"They act like she just passed away," Mom says, still trying to make sense of it all. "It's been months."

But the three of us know that isn't how dying works. When someone dies, they do it over and over again, in little ways and in big ways. You'll feel it all at once one minute, then in little drips and drops the next.

It's hard to get over losing Dad when he dies every day in my head.

"Here," I say, pulling the tag off one of the sweatshirts. "Have a hoodie."

Mom takes the sweatshirt from me, dejected. She smiles when she unfolds it, though. I understand when she puts it on. It has ears.

"Bet you didn't know you needed a black cat hoodie in your life, did you?" I say, taking my own and tossing one to Delia.

"Let's see if they have any more," Mom says. "This place is freezing."

We roll the cart full of chips and chocolate snacks to the checkout aisle, knowing full well that when Mom says "This place is freezing," what she's really saying is "There's something very wrong with this town."

CHAPTER 5

I'm surprised to be relieved when we roll back into the parking space behind Natural Grocer. In the daylight, the place *almost* looks charming, with its corny sign and faux shutters framing the windows on the outside. The apartment is grubby and sad, but I suppose anything is better than being in the Food Barn. At least there's no one here to stare at us.

Delia doesn't match my optimism. She grumbles as she looks for a place to set up her record player. I thought it was weird when she packed it in the car with us and not storage, but now I'm grateful to see something that reminds me more of home. Still, there's one dresser to share between us, and that appears to be the only flat surface in our tiny room.

I have no choice. I have to claim it.

"Dibs!" I call out, blowing off a thick puff of dust that had been caked on the dresser.

"Pip, that's the only flat surface!"

"Not true," I argue, gesturing to our feet. "There's also the floor."

"It's my *vinyl*," Delia says indignantly. "I'm not stashing my records on the floor."

"I need more room for my equipment," I say, opening my metal case and pulling out my computer and headphones.

"Besides, you had your record player strewn out on the floor in our old house. This is no different."

"*Girls!*"

Mom appears in our bedroom doorway holding what looks like a folding TV tray. She hands it to Delia, ready to make amends between us. "You are now the proud new owner of a customized record player and receiver stand," she says to her.

Delia looks unsure. "Where do I put my vinyl?"

"For now? In a suitcase under your bed."

"But—"

"I'll make you a deal," I promise her. "I'll look into pet-sitting gigs or something. First thing I can afford, I'll buy you a surface to put your vinyls on. *Capeesh?*"

Delia pouts and shrugs. She has no other choice.

"Capeesh," she agrees.

Delia steps out of our room for water. When she returns, she's holding an old, dusty cup with room-temperature tap water and a bunch of clipped ads for the Food Barn and some newspaper. I can't remember the last time I'd seen a real newspaper—I had to do a newspaper report in fourth grade for Mr. Gupta, and even then I'd printed off some article I'd found on the internet.

But I suppose if anyone was the definition of "old-school," it was Cousin Marcia. I guess I just would've expected the real estate agent and estate lawyer to have had enough sense to throw out the clippings.

Delia, with seemingly nothing else to do, unfolds Cousin Marcia's newspaper on her bed and gasps.

"Pip, look!"

I follow her finger to a spot in the *Raven Brooks Banner.* She points to a photo of a face, and I'm surprised to realize that I actually know the person in this strange place. It's the man with the salt-and-pepper goatee and gleaming white teeth from the billboard.

The words above his picture read:

"November first," Delia says, and it's a date that's emblazoned in my brain forever. "I wonder what happened to him."

I wonder what happened to him is right. The date on the newspaper page reads November 1 of last year.

"I hope he's okay," I say, because really, what else is there to say about someone I don't know?

I continue unpacking some things (as in, a pair of sneakers, an old tennis racket, some more sound equipment chords), when there's a knock at the door. Delia and I both perk our ears up, then stare at each other. We're like meerkats on the nature channel. The two of us quietly pad our way out to see Mom, who seems to be doing the same thing.

Delia is the first one to speak.

"Should we answer it?" Delia whispers.

Another knock, this one louder.

"No," I reply.

What if it's the kimchi-counter guy? Back to get his revenge with delicious, spicy probiotics?

A third knock, and this time, I hear someone clear their throat impatiently.

Mom goes to the door first but still doesn't open it.

"Hello?" she says. "Who is it?"

"Town maintenance," says a voice behind the door.

Maintenance. How ubiquitously vague.

Still, that answer is good enough for Mom (and I admit maintenance *is* something this apartment desperately needs), so she opens the door. Filling the entire doorway is indeed a big burly dude but not kimchi-counter dude. His coveralls bear a badge reading SWIFTY MOVERS.

Mom gathers herself.

"You must be the movers!" she says. *All our stuff is here!* Then a thought occurs to her.

"Hey, how was your drive here? You didn't, uh—have any problems, right?"

A tiny flicker of hope ignites inside of me. Maybe Mom has figured out a way for us to be able to leave Raven Brooks. Maybe all we need now is an actual path out.

The man's bald head scrunches into a thousand confused crinkles.

"I mean," Mom seeks to clarify, "I . . . well, we weren't able to find the road back to the highway yesterday."

The man continues to stare Mom down.

"Ma'am, your movers brought your stuff days ago. It's been waiting in the warehouse here."

"Oh," Mom says, looking as deflated as I feel. Maybe she didn't have a new idea for how to leave. She was just hoping the road out would lead us somewhere else.

Surprisingly, the Swifty guy isn't done explaining, though he's still looking at us like we're total newbs.

"This month's seismic testing," he says. "Nobody comes or goes during testing. Not safe."

And to put a disgusting period on it, he hocks the biggest loogie the world has ever seen over the side of our railing.

"I'm gonna vomit," I mumble before retreating to our room.

The movers (or rather, the storage guys?) finish bringing our things up in five trips. There are only two of them—loogie dude and another guy who doesn't speak. Only after they've driven the moving truck away do I realize I have absolutely no memory of packing.

Our last days at home were a paradox of too slow and too fast. Important moments I felt like I should be committing to memory—saying goodbye to our house, watering the rosebush I planted one last time, eating our final Noah's Pizza—all went by in a blur. But the worst moments—stumbling across Dad's favorite David Bowie record, remembering too late that we'd forgotten to take our mezuzah from the doorway, accidentally finding a photo of Ally, Stella, and me when we were friends and Ally's dad hadn't lied—those moments are all emblazoned on my brain forever.

The packing went too fast. I don't remember any of it. When Mom and Delia and I are left to stare at the contents of our life—contents that can fit in the tiny living room of Cousin Marcia's apartment—a heavy realization sets in. This is how much that's left of us.

None of us says a word as we grab our individual boxes and go about finding homes for the things we've kept.

Delia and I are in our bedroom when she breaks the silence.

"I can't believe we own a grocery store," she says. "It's kind of . . . random, right?"

"Look on the bright side: Whenever you want a midnight snack, all you'll have to do is go downstairs to the store. I mean, once Mom gets it up and running. And not full of poop chocolate," I quickly add.

But that was the wrong thing to say, apparently. Delia's chin crumples, and her lip trembles, and before I can register what's happening, tears are pouring down her face.

I don't ask. I just guide her to bed and wait.

After a moment, she wipes her face roughly and swallows. "Sorry."

"Why?" I ask. It's sort of a rule in our family; we don't apologize for crying.

She offers me a watery smile. "Dad used to bring me midnight snacks."

The familiar needle to my heart. The sting of pain against an unhealed wound.

"I didn't know that," I say, my own form of apology, and she waves me off even though I still feel bad.

"You didn't know," she says. "It was just something between him and me. Because I never used to eat enough at dinner."

I nod. She was always the kid who was in too much of a hurry to get back to whatever had absorbed her before dinner. Delia only has patience for the important stuff. Personally, I think eating is pretty important.

I feel like I owe her a secret of my own.

"He used to give me the butt of the challah," I admit.

Delia's sadness slips under utter betrayal.

"Liar! There's no way! He always ate it himself!"

I shrug. "Sometimes he did. Sometimes he sneaked it to me."

Friday-night challah was a Shabbat battle to the death. That eggy, bready, salty goodness was just too good *not* to fight over it. And the knot at the end—the butt of the braid, as we affectionately referred to it—is the prized piece. At first, Dad would tell us it was Jewish tradition that the father would eat the last piece; when I discovered there was no such tradition, he started slipping me hush money in the form of carbs.

Delia's watery smile returns, and the pain around my heart throbs, then fades.

We both understand this is the way now, this crying over nothing, this anger out of nowhere. This is how we find each other, crying over a biography of Ada Lovelace, raging at a box of cereal. Our new reality makes no sense, and instead of fighting it, it's like all three of us—me, Delia, and Mom—have simply given in to the madness of it. Like we're each leading each other, blindfolded, into a thick fog, taking turns being the lead, each groping for answers through the mist.

"I'm going to see if Mom needs help cleaning," I say, nudging Delia's foot gently.

"I'm going to wallow in the state of the world," she says melodramatically.

Mom isn't in the kitchen like I thought she was. She must be in the store.

It may have been the boxes of our things heaped in a small pile in our living room. It may have been Delia's sudden tears. Maybe it's the sudden isolation, without a working phone or a single friend to text if I had one. Whatever it is, I'm suddenly aware of just how unmoored I am. Like my anchor has slipped and sent me adrift, and I'm at the mercy of a churning ocean.

I'm breathing hard before I know it, and then my hands are on my knees. I'm hyperventilating.

Slow breaths, I tell myself. *In for three, out for four.*

Isn't that what the grief counselor had told me in those earliest days after Dad died? *In for three counts, out for four.*

In, two, three. Out, two, three, four.

When I stand from my crouch, I have to do it slowly. Too fast and I might black out.

I have no idea how I've managed it, but when my vision stops swimming, I realize I've walked to the end of Old Farm Road, a good thirty feet from 57½ and the contents of my new life.

Now that I'm away from it, my breathing has slowed.

What if I crossed the street?

I walk another block. I'm alone. And for the first time since arriving in Raven Brooks, I can feel the tiniest bit of warmth hitting my back. I can feel the heat touch my bare legs. I didn't realize that I so desperately needed the vitamin D.

It isn't long before I've walked far enough away to lose sight of 57½ Old Farm Road altogether. I know I should have told someone I was leaving, but I wasn't planning on it. And now that I'm this far away, I can't seem to make myself turn back. Not yet.

The quiet of the street is intoxicating, like the world has been cleared away just for me. I can hear the wind on the air, the distant chirp of birds (hopefully not crows), the rustle of leaves on the trees in people's yards. I reach the end of the next block and find a road sign reminiscent of those cute Victorian neighborhoods. The ornate pole holds a stack of neatly painted signs, each pointing in a different direction. Someplace called "The Square" points me back the way I came. Another sign indicates someplace called Old Town is nearby, just a quarter mile to the right. In the same direction is the Raven Brooks Station of Weather and Meteorology. And straight ahead, five hundred feet away and calling me like a siren, is a magical place called St. Nick's Lovely Llamas.

"Oh, there is no way I'm *not* going to see this," I find myself saying out loud.

I walk the five hundred feet, but I'm disappointed to find that the llama farm is fenced off, and while I can certainly *smell* the llamas, I'm separated from them by at least three run-down sheds and another high fence.

I walk along the row of wooden slats looking for one that

might have broken away or weakened. It's not that I actually have any intention of sneaking in . . . but intentions are funny things.

Clearly, I'm not the only one who's ever thought of it. There, carved deeply into the wood and smoothed by years of weather, is evidence of a similar criminal mind.

NICKY AND AARON

"Wonder how much trouble you two got up to," I whisper to the scratched names. "Bet Delia and I could give you a run for your money."

I don't notice at first that the birds have stopped chirping. I only realize it when I hear the rumble of an engine approaching from far away.

Then it's not far away at all. It's right at the end of the road.

A truck, kicking up enough dirt on the asphalt to create a cloud around it. There's a glare on the windshield, making it look like the truck is driving itself.

It idles at the far end of the road, engine growling.

I know it's ridiculous, but I can't shake the feeling that the truck is staring at me.

"Go away," I whisper, resenting the interruption to my solitude.

But when it doesn't go away, my irritation turns to fear.

Then the truck begins to drive closer.

I turn immediately, walking to the edge of St. Nick's llama farm and then to the end of the fence line. I sneak a look over my shoulder, but it isn't necessary. I can hear the engine's rumble growing closer.

"It'll pass," I tell myself.

It's just driving slowly. I'm being paranoid. It'll pass me and I'll have the street to myself again.

It doesn't, though. Instead, the truck rumbles to an idle once again, pausing halfway down the street, close enough for me to feel the sidewalk vibrating under my feet.

I pick up the pace and round the corner the only way the road curves. What I find around the corner is even less comforting than the creeping truck behind me.

There, yawing before me like an unhinged jaw, is a wide, dense expanse of forest.

I skid to a stop, ready to abandon my course, but just as I'm about to reverse direction and sprint back toward Old Farm Road, I hear the growl of the stalking truck creeping around the corner. I can just see the glint of its bumper when I turn toward the forest and sprint.

I can't see more than two trees deep, and I swat away some low-hanging branches just in time to hear the rumble of the truck's engine roar to life, picking up speed as it rounds the corner. I keep running until I think I'm sufficiently covered by the trees, then back up to a tree trunk and pivot to look through the spaces in the leaves.

The truck is still rumbling, but it's gone back to idling, sitting motionless in the middle of the street. I grip the bark of the trunk and frantically try to plan my next move.

If the door swings open, I think, *if the driver climbs out, I'll run.*

I'll just keep running until I'm deep enough into the woods

that he can't find me. Or I'll climb a tree. Sure, I haven't done that since I was nine, but sheer terror has a way of making those things come back to you.

"One, two, three . . ." I count the trees between me and the road's edge. There are at least twelve.

He can't see me, I reassure myself. *There's no way he can see me all the way back here.*

But the truck isn't moving. It isn't getting closer, but it isn't going away, either. The driver isn't getting out, but then, why is he just . . . lingering?

He's waiting for me.

My mind is racing. What will I do when the sun goes down? What if he's still there?

I'm all on my own.

Then, just as I'm gathering the courage to wait out the stalking truck, the woods that shelter me seem to change.

Sound evaporates like rain on a desert floor, and I don't want to believe it at first, but even the rustling of leaves seems to leave me behind.

It's just the sound of the truck's engine, I think. *I can't hear anything over that.*

But I know that's not it.

I try hard not to breathe, terrified that even an exhale could attract the attention of whatever I'm now certain is stalking me. A white cloud forms in front of me, hot breath on cool forest air. When it dissipates, I notice for the first time what I missed because I was too busy hiding from the truck.

There, inches from my face on an adjacent tree trunk, is the crudely carved image of the bird man. His long, scraggly feathers fall limp from his limbs; his neck bent and long, a warped question mark. His beak curved like a scythe, pointed to a tip on the end.

I know the truck is still there, waiting for me halfway down the street. But I'm not worried about the truck anymore. Because I'm being watched from a closer distance now.

It's behind me.

I turn so slowly, I wring the remaining air from my lungs, but I'm not sure I'll ever regain it. I can't imagine inhaling. It's all I can do to turn my head.

The mist that hangs between the trees does its best to hide whatever it is I can feel, but it doesn't do enough. There, no more than thirty feet away and standing over six feet tall, is the shadow of something that isn't a tree, that isn't overgrowth. I can't even be sure it's a person. In the forest's tricks of dark and light, the form is twisted and distorted, too obscured to see fully. But I'd swear I can make out a long, curved neck. I'd swear I can make out gnarled strips of feather-like tendrils hanging limp from limbs.

The acrid smell of burning fills my sinuses.

Suddenly, my feet are pounding the forest floor. I weave between tree trunks and break free of the tree line before I know what I've done. I am a sitting duck in the middle of the dead-end street, caught between whatever stalks me in the forest and whatever stalks me out here.

Except the truck has vanished.

I don't wait to consider where it might have gone. I don't turn to see if the thing from the forest has followed me out. I don't do anything but run as fast and as far as my feet will carry me, up the empty road and around the corner to the edge of St. Nick's Lovely Llamas farm, straight down one avenue to another, past the charming little stacked sign, running so fast and so hard that I think my lungs might seize.

I'm so in the grip of my panic, I nearly fly right past the Natural Grocer. Only when I've reached the end of the property line do I chance a look behind me. I don't know what I expect to see. But I don't trust my eyes at first.

They show me nothing. No pursuing truck, no lurking shadow. Nothing.

I'm once again alone and wrapped in the quiet solitude of the street I felt so eager to get away from not so long ago. Now I want to be back in the cramped little apartment so badly, I make my burning legs carry me up the steps two at a time.

I hardly have time to feel relief, though, because at the top of the stairs, blocking the tiny landing that leaves only room enough for the door to swing open, is a cardboard box. Scrawled across the top in big black letters is a simple message:

I open the front door and edge the box inside the apartment with my foot, too exhausted to crouch and lift it.

"I kept telling Mom you were in the bathroom," Delia hisses to me. "She's going to think you have dysentery."

"I—" I can't speak. All I can do is drag myself to the kitchen and drink my body weight in water. I'm filling my third cup when I return to the living room and see Mom has come back.

I'm all ready to explain that I don't have dysentery, but no explanation seems necessary. They've already moved on to a new mystery: the box.

"So . . . should we?" asks Delia. "Open it, I mean?"

"Who are we to argue with a box?" I reply.

I'm strangely grateful for the distraction. Now safely back in the apartment, the fear of earlier is dissipating. Who knows? By tonight, I might even be able to convince myself I imagined the whole ordeal.

I'm beginning to wonder how many oddities Raven Brooks expects me to simply forget.

"I'll do it," Mom says, creeping up on the package like it's a jack-in-the-box.

Mom unfolds the flaps, glares at the contents with some confusion, then begins unpacking the items, laying them out on the floor in a line. There's three smartphones, a tray of little brown balls covered in clear plastic, and a folded note.

Delia and I immediately grab the phones.

"Dibs on the green one," she says, snagging the one with the sea-foam case.

"Purple," I say, grabbing the one nearest to me. Mom takes the one with the yellow case.

"Ugh. Needs a passcode," I mutter. We were *this* close to gaining access to the outside world.

Mom lifts an edge of the plastic over the brown balls, releasing a sweet aroma into the air. Then she unfolds the note and reads out loud:

Enjoy the persimmon cookies.
My dad made them. The phones will only
work in Raven Brooks. Passcode is
CROW. Change it as soon as you unlock.
We'll find you tomorrow at school.
—A Friend.
P.S. - It's November 2nd

Delia and I look up from our phones and turn to Mom, whose fingers freeze mid-pinch into the tray of cookies.

"November . . . second?" I say, my voice losing its way at the end.

Mom keeps staring at the letter. She can only nod.

"As in . . . ?" Delia says, but she loses her way, too.

None of us needs to say it.

November 1 is the day Dad died eight months ago. Which would make today . . . the day after.

"Is that someone's idea of a sick joke?" I ask, my insides curling up in a tight ball.

"But how could anyone else know that?" says Mom.

"Um, can we talk about how this note from some random weirdo just told us that today is a day it absolutely is *not*?" says Delia, abandoning her phone. I'm still holding mine, even though I can barely feel my hands.

Even as every logical fiber of my being is screaming that this is impossible, that it couldn't possibly be November 2 because November 2 already happened, not to mention all the days in between then and July. And yet, events from the last couple of days keep nagging at me:

The date printed on the newspaper.

The way the grocers acted like Cousin Marcia died days ago instead of months ago.

The unseasonably cold weather.

The sweaters in the store.

"Maybe that culvert really was a wormhole," Delia mutters.

"Let's just pretend that's true," I say, and both Mom and Delia scoff.

"I'm not saying it is," I say. "But good to know you both think I've lost it."

Delia looks down, but Mom just goes back to staring at the note.

"I'm saying *if* that's true, then everyone in town seems to be under the same impression. Everyone," I say, holding up my phone, "except for this 'friend.'"

"Okay, so that's where we'll get answers," Delia says.

"Right," I say. "Apparently, at school tomorrow."

This gets Mom's attention.

"Oh, no. No way. You two aren't going anywhere."

"But—" I start to object.

"I'm not letting you girls out of my sight until we get to the bottom of this."

"I think mine's broken," Delia says, tapping the screen of her phone and frowning.

"What do you mean 'broken'?"

She shows me the phone, its error message indicating it can't reach a simple search engine.

I realize that I can't reach the same search engine, either. I try a different site, but I get the same thing. *Page Not Found.*

"Is the only available network RB1-Guest?" says Mom, now squinting at her own screen.

"Yeah." I fiddle with the settings a little more, but no matter what I do, the only option is RB1-Guest—Raven Brooks 1, and with no access to an app store, the only applications available seem to be the ones already preprogrammed onto the phone.

"What the heck is ChatterBack?" Delia says.

"Oh," Mom says, still squinting. "I thought it was one of those new social medias I've never heard of because I'm too old."

Upon closer inspection, it appears that every icon is a proprietary application, close to the real thing, or the thing we're used to, but special just to Raven Brooks: TikCaw; Seeker, with a blue bird; Facebrooks.

And I'd venture a bet that they only work inside Raven Brooks, too.

"It's like they built a wall around their entire electronic infrastructure," I posit.

"Just like the wall around the town," says Delia.

Suddenly, a yellow dialogue bubble appears on my phone beside a faceless avatar in the same ChatterBack yellow as the icon.

Change your password!

I drop my phone at the sight of the message, and Mom rushes to pick it up.

"Okay," she says, collecting the three of them protectively. "That's enough of the creepy-message-y phones."

I at least convince her to let us change the passwords as directed before she stashes the phones in the drawer of her bedside table.

Mom sniffs the cookies and tries a bite. After she's determined they're safe, she lets us eat them. I've never had a persimmon cookie before (hasn't anyone in this town heard of normal stuff, like chocolate chip?), but even I admit they're delicious. Delia and I devour them in two bites.

"I should have told you they were poisoned," Mom says, licking her fingers to savor the last bite of her share.

"Worth it," I reply. I don't bring up how they're even better than the bakery we used to go to on Saturdays. We don't need another memory of life with Dad today.

That night, I lie in bed on my side, looking down at the street from my window.

"Would you think I was weird if I said I wanted to go to school tomorrow?" Delia asks out of nowhere. I thought she was already asleep.

"I thought you were weird before that," I say.

She sighs, so I roll over to face her.

"I get it," I say, softening my tone so she knows I'm not mocking her.

"I just want . . ."

I wait to let her finish, but when she doesn't, I help her out.

"You just want normal."

She nods, her smile sad. Too sad for an eleven-year-old. "I just want normal."

As though that tiny confession was all it took to unburden her for the night, Delia drifts off to sleep minutes later, the sound of her quiet snoring filling the tiny room.

Delia is small, not like Mom and me. I'm tall for my age, with broad shoulders, and feet that Dad used to say I could ski on. I take after Mom. But Delia is like Dad, with her thick curls and slim build. Her hands are so tiny, sometimes I don't feel them when they reach for mine. I won't ever admit it to her, but I hope she never stops doing that.

Certain Mom must still be awake, I tiptoe to her room, but somehow she's managed to pass out, too. I'm the only one too keyed up to fall asleep.

I know I shouldn't. It's a bad idea. It might not even be safe.

None of that knowing stops me, though. As quietly as I can, I slide Mom's bedside drawer open and carefully retrieve the phone with the purple case.

I slink back to my room like a burglar and let the screen light up as I unlock it with my new passcode: Mr. Badger. The yellow message bubble is still sitting there, waiting for a response.

And even though there are a thousand reasons why I shouldn't, I answer the message back.

Done.

Simple, neutral, and to the point. My heart races as I stare at what I've done, unsure of what sort of Pandora's box I've opened, but I need the answers so badly.

I rest my phone on my stomach and pull the covers up to my chin, finally ready to doze off now that I've at least tried making contact with this friend (?).

I'm nearly asleep when I feel the phone buzz back to life. The phone glows in a rectangle underneath my thin blanket. I uncover it, fully expecting a new message from my friend. But the blank avatar picture is gone. In its place is a new picture.

A different sender.

No matter which way I try to angle the phone, I can't make out the shadowy silhouette that occupies the little avatar square beside this new message. And no matter which way I turn it, I can't escape the feeling that the shadow looks eerily familiar . . . like one I've seen not more than thirty feet from me in a thick, misty forest.

And while the picture is unsettling, the message chills me to my core.

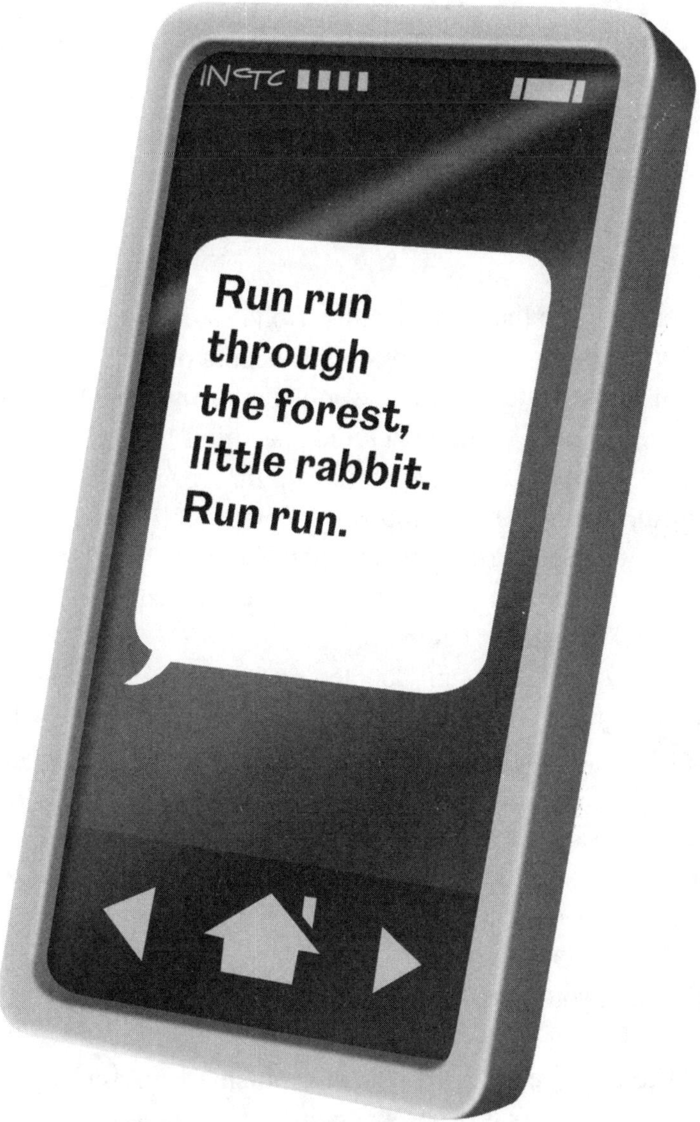
IN℃TC
Run run
through
the forest,
little rabbit.
Run run.

CHAPTER 6

When I was up the next morning, Delia is still asleep. I tiptoe out of her room and find Mom snoozing on the couch. She must have gotten up at some point in the night and launched herself here. I take a look at her and take all of her in. My mom used to be so firm and snappy, like a puma ready to devour its next meal. As I hear her melodically snore, I realize this may be the first time I see her as a *person*, not just Mom. There's a softness to her that wasn't there before—or maybe there's a softness to *me* that wasn't there before.

I head back to our room, double-check to make sure Delia is still asleep, and retrieve the phone I'd taken in the night. Its last ominous message flashes like lightning in my brain, and when I read it again, I'm surprised to find that it's disappeared, along with the message exchange with my "friend."

I'm so engrossed in finding the message that I don't register Delia's body stirring.

Then I hear Delia's voice.

"You took your pho—" she starts to say.

"Shh!" I scold her.

But Mom is already up, and in this too-small apartment, it's a matter of seconds before she's at our door, opening and closing her mouth a few times to rid herself of the morning gumminess.

"Sorry we woke you," I say, doing my best to cover my tracks. Delia side-eyes me, and I widen my own at her threateningly.

Suddenly, Mom is wide awake.

"What time is it?" she asks, looking around in a panic.

"Ask Piper to check her ph—" Delia starts, and I nudge the inside of her knee.

"Around seven. Why?" I reply helpfully.

Mom's eyes go round. "You girls need to get ready for school!"

Delia and I are back on the same team. The confused team.

"But you said—"

"I know, I know," Mom says impatiently, springing to her feet and rushing to the kitchen to dump cereal into bowls and splash oat milk over the top. "But I got to thinking last night, and it might be a good idea. Plus, I think the real estate agent pre-registered you. Now that I think about it, she did ask for both of your transcripts."

Delia doesn't wait for more of an explanation. She rushes to the bathroom instead. But I'm still wondering where Mom's change of heart came from.

"So, you don't think it's . . . dangerous?" I ask. I could tell her about the message from last night. About the truck and the shadow and the smell of something burning. I could tell her all of it. But then I remember that softness—that vulnerability—cloaking her sleeping body, and maybe, just maybe, it's better that she doesn't know.

Mom looks down at the floor before looking at me. She shrugs sheepishly. "Pip, I'm not going to lie," she says slowly. "I have no idea. About any of this."

That doesn't make me feel better.

"But the way I see it," she continues, "I'd feel safer with you girls at a school than alone in this apartment."

I pick up on the word she hoped I wouldn't.

"Alone?" I repeat. "Mom? Where are *you* going?"

Mom doesn't answer me. She does motion for me to sit on one of the old, musty kitchen chairs, and passes me a bowl of cereal that my rumbling stomach no longer wants to eat. She scrambles to the couch where she fell asleep, untangles a ton of paper she'd probably been poring over before hitting the z's, and returns to the table.

My eyes dart to the papers. It's the contents of her "Moving to Raven Brooks" binder. Or whatever's left of it—it looks thumbed-through so many times in the night, it's crumbly and old, kind of like everything else in Cousin Marcia's apartment. Mom pulls out the library card with its little Post-it that reads *USE ME!* still screaming at us in black marker.

"I'm going to the library," she says.

"How very Hermione of you," I reply. "But . . . why?"

Mom waves off my confusion. "I know, I know. I can't explain it, really," she says, and this gets my attention because I'm usually the one to follow my gut feelings, not Mom. "I just keep getting the sense that there's a missing piece to the puzzle. And if I can find the piece, I can figure out why everything around here seems so . . ."

"Off?" I suggest, which doesn't even come close to accurate, but it's good enough for Mom. She sighs and scoots closer to me at the table. Her hands are suddenly around my cheeks, and I can hear my cereal crunching in my ears. I swallow quickly so I can listen. Her eyes bore into mine.

"Pip, I need you to listen to me. I don't know what's going on here. I wish I did, believe me. But I do know this—I will never *ever* let anything happen to you or to your sister. Ever. I am going to find out what this town's . . . thing . . . is, and if we really aren't safe here, I will find a way to get us out."

I nod my head. Just once, but it's enough. It's enough for my mom to know I heard her. And I believe her.

Giving up on my cereal, I migrate to the bathroom to brush my teeth while Delia finishes up her marathon shower. I'll be lucky to get three seconds of hot water, but my mind is so entrenched in other thoughts, it barely matters anymore. Even Delia's voice catches me off guard.

"What if no one likes me?" she whispers after spitting out her toothpaste.

"Maybe no one will," I reply, not in the mood to discuss these things. But then I see Delia's bottom lip quiver, and my Big Sister instincts take over. "But they'd be incredibly wrong."

BIG SISTER INSTINCTS

I'll protect you! Against my better judgment!

"Easy for you to say," she says. "You don't care if no one likes you."

It's not true, but Delia thinks just because I'm quiet, I don't care. It's weird how silence can be mistaken for confidence.

"So, don't you care, either," I say, mustering up all that BSE, or, Big Sister Energy. "They'll never get to see your vinyl collection or learn how to do that braid you do or make your secret cashew-cream pasta."

"It's not a secret. It's just extra cashews," she mopes.

"Look, we're gonna show up to school, and everyone's going to stare at us like we have three heads, but pretty soon, nobody will care about the two new kids because there'll be some other ridiculous drama to focus on, or a science fair or something, so just try not to care."

Okay. So it's more of a pep talk for *me*. Delia doesn't need to know that.

But I'm pretty terrified of school. Everything else in Raven Brooks has been weird. What's their public education system like? And I can't pretend like I'm stoked to go to school in what should be July.

When Delia scurries out of the bathroom, I slather some moisturizer on my face. *Try not to care*, I tell myself. *Try. Not. To. Care.*

* * *

If I'd known how short the walk to school would be, I would have spent a little more time on my hair. I couldn't find my favorite pomade, so I had to use Delia's gel, which is too sticky, and now I can't run my hands along the shaved sides of my head, which is basically my only coping mechanism when I get nervous. I changed my sweater at the last minute from purple to gray, and now my lip gloss is the wrong color, and maybe my jeans are too ripped, and the little gold hoop at the top of my ear is sticking out all weird today.

If Raven Brooks is odd, Raven Brooks Middle is, well . . . normal. Bright green squares of grass line the sidewalk leading onto the grounds, and kids camp out on various patches in the quad, some sharing breakfast burritos and fruit, others lightly tossing a football back and forth.

I take a sigh of relief. This isn't the strangest thing in the world. But Delia disagrees.

"Nobody looks like me," she whispers.

"Too bad for them," I whisper back. I feel her hand snake into mine and squeeze it once as we enter the courtyard, bracing ourselves.

Every. Head. Turns.

"Just keep walking," I say through gritted teeth.

Then, with zero warning and the speed of an awkward gazelle, a boy about a hundred feet tall lunges in front of us. He's holding a microphone at arm's length, wired to a recording box he's holding by a handle in the other hand. It looks like he's conducting an interview.

"Hi! Um . . . cute girl with the purple hair!" he calls out, and I realize he means me.

"We'll edit in your name later," he says, raising the

microphone higher. "What are your thoughts about the Skokie Sasquatch?"

"Um." I blink.

"C'mon, the Skokie Sasquatch. Don't tell me you haven't heard of it."

I am utterly frozen. This is the first kid to speak a single word to us since the moment we stumbled onto the campus of our new school, and it's like he's speaking a language I can't understand. I want desperately to give him the answer he's looking for, but I can't.

So, I blink again. Now he probably thinks I have a weird eye twitch.

"Hang on," Delia chimes in excitedly. "Are you talking about that massive gorilla in Illinois? The one everyone says escaped from the zoo like twenty years ago?"

The boy shifts his microphone and his attention to Delia. "*Ten* years ago, and an *alleged* gorilla that *allegedly* escaped."

I turn to Delia. "How on earth do you know about that?"

"How do you *not*?" she asks like I'm a moron.

"Don't tell me you believe that zoo propaganda," the kid says, dropping his microphone in disappointment.

"I mean, it's a little easier to believe than a Sasquatch story," Delia replies.

"That's exactly what they want you to believe!" the boy says, his eyes growing wild. They're the deepest brown I've ever seen. They might as well be black.

"Who's *they*?" asks Delia. She has this way of getting a rise out of total strangers. I'd stop her, but it's too entertaining.

"I take it you've never seen my show," the boy replies, and I stifle a laugh. It's clear whoever this kid is, he takes his "work" very seriously.

Before we can ask him any follow-up questions (or slowly back away . . . I'm still debating), he fishes two *actual* business cards out of the carrying case for his recorder.

"Vinod Reddy," he says, as though it's totally normal to introduce yourself like you're a grown-up.

His card reads:

Vinod Reddy
Host and Producer of ALLEGEDLY
The Truth is Hiding in Plain Sight.

New episodes every Tuesday.
www.SeeMe.rb1/ALLEGEDLY

I look up at Vinod, who is eagerly awaiting our response.

"It's a three-time Ravie nominee."

Don't ask what a Ravie is, I silently plead Delia, and I swear she heard me because she sticks her hand out instead.

"Delia Tillman. This is Piper. She's more of a watcher than a talker," Delia says, and Vinod nods and together they immediately start debating the plausibility of the Skokie Sasquatch. I'm struck by how my sister can slip right into any social situation as though she belongs there. As it turns out, she was worried for nothing.

Luckily, Vinod seems like the inclusive type. I'm willing to bet he's never met a person he hasn't tried to make a friend, and I have to admire that about him.

"So, listen," Vinod says after he and Delia have wrapped up. He eases himself between my sister and me, draping an arm over each of our shoulders like we've known each other forever. "I know you probably haven't gotten the warmest welcome."

"You could say that," Delia replies.

"Don't take it personally. We don't get many new folks around here," he replies.

"I mean, just a theory," I say, "but it may have to do with the enormous brick wall that surrounds this whole town." I leave out the guard birds. Oh, and the garage lady. And the angry mob. And the truck and the shadow. And the weird phones. And the texts. Whatever.

I feel like Vinod might already know about at least some of that, though, because for the first time since meeting him, he looks uncomfortable. His arms slip off of our shoulders, and as the bell rings, he's suddenly in a hurry to get to class like everyone else.

Still, he's too considerate to leave us completely abandoned.

"What grade are you in?" he asks Delia.

"Sixth."

He points to the far corner of the quad, toward a hall marked by the silhouette of a small black bird. (Of course.)

"Sixth is in there. You should go to the head office at the end of the hall. Ask for Ms. Park. She's the nice one."

Delia thanks Vinod and gives me one more "good luck" squeeze of the hand before hurrying toward the hall.

Vinod turns his focus to me.

"Eighth," I say, answering his question before he asks.

"Got a schedule?"

I shake my head. *My schedule is that it's July,* I want to say, but don't.

He smiles, and just like that, the Vinod from earlier returns.

"Then you're with me. You can't exactly crash a school class, you know? What are they going to do, suspend you for learning? I'm joking—they wouldn't. First period is history with Mr. Dork."

I guess Vinod is right. Not like I'm risking much. But did he say. . . ?

"I'm sorry, Mr. D—"

"Don't." Vinod holds up his hand. "He has zero sense of humor. Less than zero. We're talking negative-number territory. It's automatic detention for even smiling at his name."

"Yikes."

"You've been warned."

Mr. Dork's classroom is barely controlled chaos. The second Vinod walks in, at least three kids try to coax him over to sit beside them, but he just waves amiably like the local celebrity he is and zeros in on one kid in the corner who isn't even bothering to wave.

She's sitting there, smiling at Vinod like they share a joke only the two of them know, and Vinod kindly makes sure there's a seat for me, too, before making his way to the corner where his friend is draped casually over her chair like a soft flannel.

It's Jess, the girl from the Food Barn.

"Hey, it's Hoodie Girl."

"Jess, Piper—new girl," says Vinod. "Piper, Jess."

"We've met," she says.

I panic and can't decide whether to nod or wave, so I do a sort of half of each and then try to right myself by noticing her pendant.

"Cool crystal," I say, pointing to the tiny light blue stone on a fine cord around her neck.

I notice that Jess has a new collection of braids thatching her hair today. This time, there are five tiny ones pulled into one master weave on each side of her head, folding under the crown and back out again over the top, forming a sort of knot at the back and exposing ears lined with rings of silver. On the toes of her boots, I notice she's drawn a collection of skulls connected by tiny vines and leaves.

"Piper doesn't know about the Skokie Sasquatch," Vinod interrupts.

"What? How can she not know about the Squatch?" asks Jess, like if someone were in disbelief I didn't know about Robin Hood or Queen Elizabeth.

"I know, right? It's impossible," says Vinod, animated until he realizes that Jess is gently mocking him. I catch it right away, though. Which is how I am now sure Jess and I are going to be friends. Sarcastic people unite!

A short, round man in a polo shirt hustles into the class barking commands before he's made it through the door.

"Books open! Page one eighty-three! We start our unit on the Greeks today!"

Then, like he has a sixth sense or something, Mr. Dork looks up, *sniffs the air*, and his eyes land on me.

"Who's that?" he barks.

That. I'm a thing.

"I'm Piper," I say with as much confidence as I can dig up.

Mr. Dork blinks at me. "Piper. And why are you in my class, Piper?"

"Um . . . I'm new," I say, trying my best to keep my voice monotone. *Don't make waves*, I tell myself. *Blend in. Act casual.*

I'm 99 percent sure this is going to end badly when Jess comes to the rescue.

"Sorry, Mr. D., what page did you say?"

Just as I'm thinking his eyes are about to vaporize me, the ancient Greeks pull Mr. Dork back to the lesson, and he pretends we never had the interaction at all. For the rest of the class,

we learn about the goddess Artemis, and I'm surprised to see that the class is just a regular class. *Phew*, I think. We could have been learning an ancient bird language for all I knew.

Vinod and I don't

SQUAWK! SQUAWK! SQUAWK!

share any more classes for the rest of the day, though he does take me to get my official schedule (provided reluctantly by a secretary with wide-rimmed glasses who was just as enthused to see me as Mr. Dork was).

Class after class, everything is the same. I walk in, the teacher stares at me, wonders who I am, someone distracts them, and then continues on. I wonder if Delia is having the same kind of day. I don't see Delia at all in the quad or at lunch. If she weren't so good at making friends, I'd be worried.

Speaking of lunch . . . when the cafeteria bell rings, I have no idea what to do. At home, Mom used to pack me bento boxes filled with lots of yummy things—sandwiches, snacks, fruit, and sometimes she'd throw something just for fun in, like a sheet of stickers or a kazoo (okay, that one didn't go over well with my former teachers). But obviously that wasn't the case now. I give three dollars to a lunch lady in a hairnet who passes me some kind of kale-and-mushroom salad. Not your typical cafeteria food, but I guess Raven Brooks Middle isn't exactly your typical school.

I lap around the cafeteria, hoping to see Vinod or maybe Jess, but they aren't there. Resigned to my solitude, I sit in the back left corner with my tray and dig in. The mushrooms are a little overcooked, but overall it's not that bad. Besides, I like kale.

When I get up to toss out my trash, I spot Jess through the window, sitting under a tree. I rush outside to see her and say hello, but she spots me first.

"How goes the first day?" she asks.

"Er," I reply, which is really the only answer I can think of to describe any of this.

"Sorry I didn't find you earlier. I usually eat lunch outside," Jess says. "At least you know where to find me tomorrow. Hey, who do you have for next period?"

I show her my schedule as the bell rings, letting us know lunchtime is over.

"Mrs. Wayneright," Jess reads, pointing to the room my schedule says is civics. "She's all right. I spilled my smoothie all over myself last year in her level-one class, and she let me go home early so I didn't have to sit in it for the rest of the period. You'll like her. Hey, after class, meet me out here." She gestures to the courtyard.

I think I've made a friend? I don't want to jinx myself but . . . Jess is the closest to "friend" I can think of. Even back home. I'd had friends, but when Dad died, they kind of . . . dissipated.

After the final bell, Jess and I meet at the courtyard where we wait for Vinod, who apparently comes outside here after school, too, and for Delia to get out of class. Apparently, Raven Brooks Middle keeps sixth and seventh through eighth grades really separate, which is why I didn't see her all day. I like Jess and Vinod, but I'm anxious to see my sister. Usually she can make me pull my hair out, but I kind of feel like I need a hug.

I don't have to wait too long for Delia, though. She barrels toward me like she's on fire.

"Pip! Pip!" she squeals. "Did you have a good day? I had a *great* day! I learned more things than I did in a year at our old school, and I think I'm going to be on the morning announcements tomorrow, and my art teacher made me do a presentation on my hair color, and—and—"

She sees my lip quiver, and I think Delia instantly knows to stop talking. Then, as if on instinct, she scoops me into a hug.

I can't help it. I sob. Right there on the courtyard. In front of everyone.

It's probably one of the most horrifying things I've ever done, and I feel like my tear ducts have betrayed me.

"Shh, shh, it's okay," Delia says, like Dad used to when we were afraid of the monsters under our beds.

Only this time, the monsters are . . . I'm not really sure.

"I'm sorry," I say to Jess and Vinod after Delia releases me. "It's been . . ."

"A lot," Jess chimes in. "We know."

"Everything will make sense soon," Vinod says, even though I wish he could stop being cryptic and tell me.

Then, as Delia and I are about to take our leave, Vinod leans in, his hand clasped in a friendly grip on mine, leaning in like we've known each other forever.

In my ear, he whispers, "Aren't persimmon cookies the best?"

He and Jess pull away so fast, I think maybe it didn't happen. But when Vinod turns, his long legs barely holding up his lanky body, he winks at me, and just like that, I feel a massive headache coming on.

"I'll message you later!" he calls out, as though it'll simply be a casual chat. As though anything about this could be casual.

So much for pretending.

* * *

The walk home is *The Delia Show*. She talks about Counselor Kim, who is without a doubt the nicest person she's ever met. She laughs about the kid in her second period who invented this dance called the "FlapJack" that's practically gone viral in Raven Brooks (since, you know, no access to the outside world and all). She tells me how there's a secret lunch lady who has good food and how for lunch she had a sandwich with Dijon mustard, how a girl named Destiny has the same obsession with her favorite K-pop star, how bearded dragons actually wave at each other, and please, please, please tune in to the morning announcements tomorrow, because she filmed the weather segment today. I don't ask her how she knows what the weather will be tomorrow.

She tells me every little thing, which should make me happy because it means she had a good first day. And I should be paying closer attention, but the best parts of my day were meeting Vinod and Jess, and thinking of them only makes me think of my former friends, Ally and Stella.

When we left our old home, like the minute we drove across the city limit, I felt like I'd cut a tether I didn't know had been choking me. Suddenly, their ignored texts and photos at parties without me didn't sting as badly. It was like all I'd needed to do for all those months was to put thirty miles of pavement between us to dull the pain of their surgical removal of me from their lives. It was just like Mom said it would be.

They were never your friends, she'd said, and I knew what she was really saying was they were never *our* friends.

89

The Dunlaps were never the "family" to us that they'd claimed to be. Sure, we'd spent Thanksgivings and Labor Days with them, taken trips to the lake and planned joint birthday parties because Ally and I were born a mere day apart. When Ally's dad and my dad went into business together, it was just so natural that cookouts would always include the Dunlaps, and that we would be invited up to the cabin anytime they went—we didn't even need to ask. When Stella moved to our town and started at our school, of course she and I became friends. She was super into music, too, and if I loved her, I knew Ally would.

They were never your friends, Mom told me over and over again, but that wasn't true. They *were* my friends. We were all friends. Which is why it was so hard to understand how Ally's dad could put all the blame on my dad. It shouldn't have come as any surprise that Ally and Stella kept forgetting to call me back after that. It still surprised me, though.

Delia's voice takes me back into the present.

"And then I was like, 'But then you never would have had bubble tea, and Destiny totally agreed I was right.'"

Delia stops walking.

"What?" I turn to see what's wrong.

"For someone who notices everything, you need to get better at pretending not to ignore people when they're talking," Delia says, her arms crossed in front of her.

"Bubble tea, Destiny said you were right, Dijon mustard. Got it."

Delia rolls her eyes, unconvinced, but she starts walking again.

Just as she passes me, though, I spot something interesting.

We're maybe thirty feet from home, and there's a fence separating the garage of one house from the garage of the next on the same side of the street. There, peeking from the partial cover of a juniper tree, is the unmistakable sketch of the bird man on the fence.

"What's going on?" Delia asks me. She can always tell when I've noticed something. My superpower. Who needs to fly or shoot laser beams from your palms when you can . . . see things?

"Yowza," Delia says, sucking in her breath. She sees it, too. "What is that, like a . . . man-bird-nightmare?"

"I dunno," I reply, running my fingers over the drawing that so closely resembles the one from the brick wall near the call box—and the one in the woods—right down to the spindly legs and talons like knives. As it turns out, the picture isn't drawn onto the fence. It's actually etched into the wood.

No, it's *burnt* into it. Like a brand.

"I would *not* want to meet the mind behind that creation," Delia says, and I turn to look at her.

"What?"

She backs up a step.

"Nothing," I reply.

I know she doesn't believe me. And I know I need to tell her what I've seen.

But not yet. Something is telling me not yet.

CHAPTER 7

We walk in the door of the apartment to find Mom exactly where we left her on the couch. Only this time, she's buried behind enough photocopies to make an entire fleet of paper airplanes.

"You are not going to believe what I found," she says.

"School was peachy awesome, thanks," I mumble, and she scowls up at me.

"Well, if I knew you were going to be so grumpy, I wouldn't have located your favorite snack to have waiting for you when you got home," she mopes, and my stomach does a little guilt flip.

"Hang on. You found—" Delia starts.

"That's right," Mom says smugly. "Of course, if you're too cool for—"

We race to the kitchen, and there, laid out gloriously on the tiny nook's table in the corner of the kitchen we're calling a dining room, is a cornucopia of Buckingham's Fruit Leather.

This was no small feat. Mom must have planned way in advance for this. Buckingham's Fruit Leather is, little did we know, a grocery staple to exactly no place outside of home, a lesson we learned immediately upon leaving there. We finally got the hint after our fourth convenience store stop that the obsession with this particular snack clearly did not extend beyond the borders of the city we'd just said goodbye to forever.

It shouldn't have been as heartbreaking as it was. But after so much heartbreak already, it's like we couldn't take one more disappointment. Delia and I broke down somewhere between the second and third night of our journey.

Mom must have made it her mission to get her hands on those fruit leathers one way or another.

After eating a fistful of them, I slink back into the living room, where Mom is once again consumed by the photocopies and open books.

I lay my head in her lap, and that seems to be enough because she gently runs her fingers through my hair the way she does when I get a headache.

"Where did you find them?" I asks.

"Indiana," she says, and I can tell she's been bursting to share her secret for a while now. "That little country market where you girls bought those gnomes. I've had them in my bag for a rainy day."

"Seriously? The gnome place?" I ask.

Mom shrugs. "I bought up their whole stock."

"You're amazing," I reply.

Mom cups my chin after she's done stroking my hair and returns to her books. I wish I could tell Mom about my day, but this is hard on all of us. Now I know it's time to discuss what she learned.

"Okay," I say, "lay it on me."

Mom takes a deep breath. Delia joins us in the living room, a small stack of fruit leathers clutched in her hand like playing cards.

"So." Mom steadies herself. "Your cousin Marcia was busy in her last days." Then she looks up at us, clearly trying to decide whether or not to share the next part.

"Spill," Delia says, and I guess that's all it takes.

"I think she knew she was going to die."

Delia's eyes go wide. "Like, psychically, or . . . ?"

Mom shakes her head. "I really don't know. What I do know is that she purposely set aside a very specific set of books."

I pick up one of the books Mom checked out.

A Birder's Guide to Magpies?"

I look at the rest of her library haul, and the titles are just as perplexingly random.

101 Ways to Craft Your Way to Happiness, The Novice Printmaker: 10 Basic Lessons, Failed Foundations: The Greatest Bridge Disasters in History, The Right Way to Drink Water.

Delia picks up the last one.

"There's a wrong way?"

I shake my head. "I don't get it. Why would Cousin Marcia have all of these set aside? It's like she just went through the library and picked a bunch of books at random."

Mom claps like I've won a prize. "Exactly!"

Then she frantically flips to one of the marked pages in the magpie book, bringing her finger down on one section in particular.

"See it?"

I squint for a moment, and there it is: the letter *F* circled lightly in pencil, and at the bottom of the page, a number: 152.

All it takes is Mom pointing out the first one, and suddenly, I'm scanning page after page for a circled letter. Some aren't letters, but numbers. Some are just punctuation marks. But every single one is paired with a number in the margin or at the bottom of the page.

I look at the stacks of photocopies.

"What's with those?"

Mom shrugs. "I didn't know what I was looking for, and the library would only let me take home six books at a time."

"So, you copied the whole book?"

"Of course not!" Mom says indignantly. "The copier gave out before I could. By the way, we're not allowed back at the library for a while."

"Awesome, making friends all over the place," I murmur.

Which reminds me of Vinod and Jess. I'm just about to tell Mom (and Delia) that Vinod is the "friend" behind our care package, but now Delia has questions.

"So, if Cousin Marcia knew she was going to die, does that mean she thought she was setting these books aside for . . . Dad?"

Mom tries to wrap her head around the question. So do I.

If that were the case, then Cousin Marcia would have had to know that Dad would take over the deed to the Natural Grocer and move to Raven Brooks to find the books she left.

Mom seems to come to the same conclusion I do. "She and your dad didn't even know each other. I can't imagine she assumed he'd get her message."

"But what *is* her message?" I ask, still examining the tiny circled letters. Now that I know they're there, my eyes can't stop searching for them. It's the worst kind of hidden-picture game.

"Maybe like a word search?" suggests Delia.

But that's too easy. And Cousin Marcia didn't circle whole words, just letters.

Then it clicks. "It's a cipher!"

Mom and Delia look at me, then at the pages, then at me again.

"Every letter means something else," I say, tapping the number in the margin. "That's what the numbers are for."

They're still looking at me.

"A cipher. C'mon, a code would be a word that means a different word; a word search would be a word that means what it means but it's just hidden. This is a cipher!"

Delia crinkles up her face. "Okay, puzzle master, it's a cipher, calm down."

I roll my eyes. "Don't be jealous."

"So, all we have to do is figure out what each letter means, and we'll see the code!" Mom says, running to grab a pad of paper and a pen. "Let's get cracking!"

But we're all stumped. That's when an idea dawns on me.

"We're missing the actual message," I say. "We can't crack the code because there's nothing to decode. That's what the numbers are for."

"You're going to need to back up a little," Mom says, rubbing her temples to ward off a headache.

"Normally with a cipher, you have a message," I say. "It just looks like a bunch of letters or symbols mashed together. You have to break the code to find out what each symbol means, and then you translate the message."

"I'm kind of understanding," Mom says, still rubbing.

"But Cousin Marcia didn't leave us a message. Instead, she left us the symbols and the numbers. We have to create the message using the numbers."

"Headache," Mom says, rubbing harder.

Delia helps me out. "The numbers show the order of the letters!"

She shuffles the pages in front of her until she finds what she's looking for. Finally, she thumps her finger down on a page with the letter *D* circled. In the margin is the number 1.

"There's our first letter."

Mom gets excited again. "Maybe it's not a cipher, then! Maybe it's just a message!"

But I already ruled that out. I hold up the book on bridge disasters, pointing to a circled symbol and its corresponding number.

"What word do you know that's spelled with a sigma?"

Mom sighs and falls back in her seat on the couch. "Why is everything in this town so . . . ?"

"Hard?" suggests Delia.

"Weird?" I try.

"I was going for secretive, but all of those work," says Mom.

I feel bad for her. She really thought she had something here. And the thing is, I think she does. I just think that whatever Cousin Marcia wanted someone to find when they pulled those books, she wanted to make sure it was the *right* someone.

I can't imagine that's us.

There are two books lying on the floor by the coffee table that look neglected. They're not earmarked or opened to reveal circled letters or symbols. They're heavy, one nearing a thousand pages, both dedicated to history. Specifically, the history of Raven Brooks.

"I am not looking forward to scanning those babies for hidden letters," I groan.

Mom looks up. "I don't think those count," she says. "They were in a different stack behind the counter. I think Cousin Marcia just included them for good measure."

"So, like, whoever took over the store would have a history lesson on the town?" I ask, cracking the tome open.

"Frankly, it's the only thing in this mess that looks remotely interesting," Mom says. "Did you know there used to be an amusement park here?"

Indeed there did. There's an entire chapter devoted to it: "The Rise and Fall of the Golden Apple Amusement Park."

"That sounds ominous," I say. "Just our luck to have missed the amusement park phase of this place. Bet that was a really fun time."

As it turns out, though, it actually *is* lucky. Apparently, the park was open for exactly one day before it killed a little girl and turned the entire town upside down. A picture of the deadly ride—a terrifyingly steep roller coaster aptly named the Rotten Core—takes up the top-left corner of the page.

Knowing that a little girl died on that very coaster makes me flinch away from staring at it for too long, but the picture beside it is a little harder to look away from. It's a man, barrel-chested with neatly parted brown hair, an argyle sweater and a wide smile. His eyes, even in the black-and-white picture, seem to twinkle with mischief. Nothing, though, can prepare me for the sharply waxed handlebar mustache curling to tiny spikes pointing straight to his nostrils. It looks like if he smiled any wider, they'd go straight up his nose and pierce his brain.

The caption below the picture reads: Theodore Peterson, Famed Park Designer.

"Let me guess," Delia says. "The park was bird-themed."

I scan the contents of the page. "Apples," I say. "Golden Apples."

Mom lifts her head, suddenly interested. "The clerk at the gnome place told me about those. Candy people. I guess they all know each other."

"They're candy?" I ask.

"*Were* candy," says Mom, and she's right.

I read from the text: "Owned by the Tavish family, they were a local favorite. Unfortunately, the business filed for bankruptcy shortly after the park disaster."

"'Disaster' is a funny way to say a girl died," says Delia.

I read on, and as it turns out, the disaster didn't end with this girl's death. Her name was Lucy Yi.

"It burned," I say.

"What do you mean 'it burned'?" says Mom, taking a break from her headache.

I read: "Local consensus seems to indicate that the Golden Apple Amusement Park succumbed to an as-yet-unsolved . . ."

I snap the book shut. "Arson."

"Whoa," says Delia. "I guess when Raven Brooks gets mad, they get *mad.*"

Immediately, the image of the angry townspeople filtering into the forest flashes across my mind.

And immediately after that, I remember the billboard.

"It's the girl from the billboard!" I say, showing the image of Lucy Yi to Mom and Delia.

I recall the words above the pictures of those five people: *No More Missing. No More Lost.*

Lucy was one of the lost.

I close the book again, trying my best to return to the texts and their hidden message.

"This is going to take an *eternity* to put together," I whine.

The odds of us cracking the code are about as good as me admitting I still have my phone, which I'm not supposed to have.

"Oh!" Mom says, and I jump because for a second, I think maybe she read my mind.

"I don't have it!" I blurt.

"What?"

"Nothing."

Mom squints at me for a minute. I'll never crack, though.

It's Delia who interrupts the standoff. "What's with the spy cam?"

She's unburying what looks to be a bundle of wires from the mountain of papers.

Mom turns her suspicions on her other daughter, and I make a mental note to thank Delia later for taking the heat off me.

"I found it in the kitchen cabinet—Delia, exactly how did you know what that was?" Mom asks.

If Delia is fazed, she doesn't show it. "Everyone knows what a spy cam is, Mom," she replies, which is not true, because I had no idea it was a spy cam.

Still, I'm going to take Delia's side. There was that time Mom put the TV remote in our refrigerator back at home.

I clear my throat. "No offense, Mom, but you're not exactly up on your, er, electronics."

She trains her eyes on me and says pointedly, "I know enough to know when one of three phones is missing from my drawer."

Yikes. Busted.

"Does that mean I can have mine?" Delia says, not waiting for an answer. She runs to Mom's room to retrieve the green one.

"I'm sorry. I just, I couldn't sleep last night, and—" I say.

Mom holds up her hand. "Save it. We'll discuss it later."

She's still too focused on Delia to deal with me.

"Exactly how much do you know about covert surveillance?"

Mom asks once Delia is back in the room, but Delia is distracted.

"Oh, you know, just the basics," Delia replies, eyes on her screen. "Hey, we got an invite from Jess to come over!" she adds excitedly.

"Who is Jess?" Mom asks, sensing she's losing control. "And who says you're going anywhere? I'm still the parent here."

I guess it's my turn to rescue Delia.

"Why would Cousin Marcia have a spy cam hidden in the kitchen cabinet?" I ask Mom.

Not only does Mom not know, it's clearly made her uneasy.

"I don't get the impression she's the one who put it there," she says. "I only found it because I was doing a deep clean of the cabinets."

I get it now. "You're the one who disabled it," I say, and now I understand her discomfort.

Aha. *Someone's been watching us.*

"Does that mean . . . ?" I start to see our cozy, run-down little apartment in a whole new light. "Could there be . . . others? Other spy cams, reporting on us?" I whisper to Mom, not wanting to scare Delia.

Mom does her best to reassure me. "I searched. If there's anything to find, I would have found it."

I want to believe Mom, but I don't know. If there's one, there's got to be more. Right?

Why would someone be spying on Cousin Marcia?

Or, more brain-racking, why would someone be spying on *us*?

Mom isn't done yet, though. "One last discovery," she says, standing from the sofa and heading for the kitchen.

I don't know what I was expecting her to reveal when she reached the kitchen, but I sure didn't expect her to stand at the wall by the sink that faces the side of the apartment that points toward the store.

She turns to Delia and me, a preamble apparently in order.

"I thought it was a little strange that the apartment didn't appear to have an internal door to the store downstairs," she says.

I gasp. She did not find a secret passage. There's no way.

Mom traces her finger along the wall until she hits the edge of the countertop. Underneath, she flips some sort of switch, and out swings . . . a hidden door.

"Yesssssss!" Delia says, pumping her fist.

"Yes, indeed," Mom says, looking mighty proud of herself.

But as I venture closer to the doorway leading to the dark wooden stairs, I stop short.

"Holy spider! Oh . . . oh, there's a lot of them."

Delia comes running. Sure enough, there's an entire family. Multiple generations. So. Many. Long-legged. Spiders.

"Ew" is all I can manage to muster. I hate spiders.

"Okay, it's not quite ready for human passage yet," Mom says.

"Unless," Delia says, her eyes glowing. "Radioactive spiders! This is my chance!"

Mom puts her arms out to bar Delia from the stairwell. "No spider experiments. No superhero transformations. I'm calling an exterminator in the morning. I just wanted to show you girls that it's here."

I nod. I feel frozen. I really, really, really hate spiders. Even thinking about them makes my stomach squirm.

"Anyway," Mom moves on, "I'm going to a town meeting tomorrow night."

"I'm sorry, a what?" I ask, struggling to make the leap from spiders and Freaked-Out Mom to Concerned-New-Citizen Mom.

"I'm going to find out what is going on with this 'seismic testing' ridiculousness," Mom replies. "The sooner they open the gates to this town, the sooner we get access to a *normal world*."

Ah. This is all a part of Mom's Operation Leave Raven Brooks.

I decide to throw Mom a bone. "It's a good idea, Mom."

She looks relieved to not be arguing anymore. And I'm relieved that she seems to have forgotten about me stealing the phone from her drawer. Win-win.

We part ways. I shoot Jess a text that we can't see her today but we'll definitely meet up in the morning before school. Then I do one of my favorite things ever and start polishing off my sound equipment. I know it sounds weird, but scraping off some dust bunnies and making them squeaky clean again is the most satisfying feeling in the world.

That night, Delia and I are busy fiddling with our phones in bed. It's taking a lot of getting used to only using these weird Raven Brooks apps. No more messages from the bird thing, which honestly, is a massive relief. At least I won't see Ally's photos of her partying or whatever.

I peruse the SeeMe app, and it takes me no time at all to find Vinod's channel. *Allegedly* is the number one show and prominently placed right there on the home page. I watch three immensely entertaining episodes more before it occurs to me that maybe he's done an episode on Raven Brooks. If not, he should. There's enough conspiracy in this town to fill a month's worth of shows, at least.

Ugh! On this whole phone, I can't find a single thing on Raven Brooks.

Then I hear Delia pipe up.

"I'm not saying that I'm going to be farting all night because of those fruit leathers," she says, breaking the rhythm of our thumb tapping, "but fair warning, I'm not saying that I'm *not* going to be farting all night because of those fruit leathers."

"Try to fart toward the wall," I tell her.

She's quiet for a little longer before she says, "Do you think Dad would know how to decipher Cousin Marcia's code?"

I freeze. That's not something I thought of.

"If he did, he certainly didn't tell us," I say. "So there's no point in wondering about the what-ifs. We're here now. We're on it now. It's our mission."

Delia nods. But she's made a really good point.

Did Dad know something about this?

My brain won't stop racing. It's like a hundred cogs just started moving that had never been going before.

I watch Delia without her noticing. How long ago was it that she was crawling into my bed with me, putting her little hand underneath my chin so she could feel the breath coming out of my nose? She said she used to do that so she'd know I was still alive. It was always hard for me to imagine a person that young worried that much. Delia puts up a good front. She has the sense of humor and charisma to fool just about everyone she meets. Nobody would know about the panic that vibrates just below the surface of her skin, the anxiety that creeps out when she's pushed to her limit.

Now, looking at her tucked tightly under her covers, her face glowing blue in the dark, her screen's light bearing down on her, I wonder how much of our new home I can keep from her before it finds its way to her.

I wonder how much I *should* keep from her.

Suddenly, a toxic fart permeates the air, filling up the cavities of my nose.

"Maybe that's the 'seismic activity' this town keeps prattling on about," I say, my contemplation halted.

"I did warn you," she says, giggling.

CHAPTER 8

The next day at school, I try to give all my attention to Mr. Dork because Artemis really is the single coolest Greek goddess with her silver bow and penchant for wild animals, but I simply can't focus because Delia and I are going over to Jess's house tonight, and Jess hasn't said two words about it since I sat down next to her and Vinod this morning.

I got another message from the bird profile at some point during Mr. Dork's class, and my stomach churns as I see it from beneath the depth of my backpack (since we're not supposed to have our phones on during lessons). It says:

You can't hide, little rabbit.

"Now, was Artemis a good goddess, or a bad goddess?" Mr. Dork asks, his hand slamming the marker into the whiteboard hard enough to make it rattle on the wall.

"Good!" someone shouts.

"Naw, she was a total baddie," says someone else.

"What? She was the protector of, like, girls and animals and stuff."

"'Girls and animals and stuff'?"

"Yeah, she was, like, you know, nurturing."

"Ow! My eyes just got stuck in the back of my head from *rolling so hard*."

"Children!" Mr. Dork interjects. "If I may interrupt."

"Hope your face sticks that way."

"What're you, five?"

"Enough!" Mr. Dork rumbles.

The class goes silent.

"If I may?" Mr. Dork pretends to ask for permission. "Thank you," he says after some silence. "Now, that was obviously a trick question," he says, making a point to shame the actual life out of the two students who argued. "Like all ancient gods and goddesses, Artemis was neither good nor bad. The deities were constructed as complex divine beings, capable of fallibility just like mortals."

He walks away from the board and starts pacing the front of the room. He's super into it. "They were subject to whims and tended to act on emotion. Now, why would that be?"

Mr. Dork says it tentatively; he's taking a risk on opening the discussion back up.

So, I take a risk and raise my hand.

He looks surprised.

"Yes, er . . . new girl."

"Piper."

"Penelope."

Close enough.

"Because if they made mistakes, it was okay for regular people to make mistakes, too," I answer.

He doesn't look like he wants to be impressed. "And therefore the gods became . . ."

He waits for the answer he's clearly expecting the class to give. He's expecting a bit much.

"*Relatable!* Come on, people!"

He's not nice, that's for sure, but Mr. Dork does know his Greek mythology, I'll give him that.

"And what would the gods need to experience in order to be relatable to humans?"

The class thinks on this.

"Hunger!"

"Anger!"

"Boredom!"

"Loss."

I'm hardly paying attention until that last one, and that's only because it comes out of Jess's mouth.

For a second she looks like she regrets saying it. Vinod looks at her like he wishes she hadn't said it.

But the rest of the class, even—and I can't believe it—Mr. Dork, looks sorry for her. They eye her with wrinkled brows, like they all share in whatever feeling she's just confessed to. But Vinod looks worried. Not about Jess, just . . . worried.

I can't stop thinking about it for the rest of the day. Not during lunch outside when I poke at my rice from the Good Lunch Lady and laugh at Vinod's latest idea for his SeeMe channel. Not during biology when we learn just how many cellular similarities we have with pigs. Not even when Coach Rockefeller heads the soccer ball straight into the goal without messing up her bangs.

By the time I'm walking out of civics with Jess and we meet up with Vinod and Delia, I've had about as much pretending as I can take.

"I have questions," I say straight to Vinod, and while I can tell he's caught off guard for a second, he regains his composure fast.

"You mean about my last episode? You know you can always ask in the comments section, it boosts my visibility, you know," he says a little too loudly, and a couple of girls passing by giggle.

"We commented, Vinod!" they say, and he laughs nervously as they sprint away.

"Yeah, not what I meant," I say, losing patience at lightning speed.

"I know what you meant," he hisses through his teeth.

"Look, we know this is a lot," Jess says.

"Oh, you do?" I ask, not meaning for all this venom to escape, but I'm just frustrated. And *of course* they can't talk about it. And *of course* my family and I are just supposed to be okay with being kept in the dark until someone who knows what the heck is going on decides it's okay to clue us in.

"I can't take this anymore!" I yell. I don't mean to yell. But whatever. Maybe I do mean to yell.

Heads are starting to turn in the quad. But I'm getting pretty used to that feeling, and I'm getting pretty used to not caring.

Jess looks around, takes quick stock of the situation, then leans in and gives me a hug tight enough to crack my back. Her voice is loud enough that everyone in the quad can hear it, but when her words come out, they still don't make sense.

"It's okay. I know you miss her so much."

"Her—?"

Vinod joins Jess, clutching me from the other side, and scoops Delia in for good measure.

"Cousin Marcia," Jess soothes.

"She was special to all of us," Vinod adds, burrowing his face into my collar.

"Uh." I try to break away, but they hold me tighter.

"It's going to be okay," Vinod says. "Just let it all out. Everyone understands. Loss is hard."

Then Jess leans into my ear and whispers. *"Don't* let it all out."

Delia squirms. "I'm so confused."

Then the girl from first period who argued for Baddie Artemis joins the hug, scooping Jess into an embrace.

"I know you understand," she says to Jess, squeezing her extra hard, and because Jess's face is literally pressed against mine, I can feel her grimacing.

"Thanks, Ruby," she says in a whisper, and I think it's because she can't fake sincerity any louder than that.

The guy who argued for Good Artemis suddenly approaches and wraps the girl, Jess, and I guess the rest of us, into a massive embrace and gives a solid one-two squeeze.

Literally *none* of this makes sense.

"We're all going to get through this," he says, and for reasons I can't fathom, Baddie Artemis girl hiccups a quick sob, and Jess grits her teeth and responds with a quick "Mm-hmm."

Just as I'm thinking I will need to scratch and claw my way out of this excruciating group hug, Good Artemis guy wrinkles up his chin and says, "They'll find him, Jess."

Then he lets go and so does Baddie Artemis Ruby, and at last, Jess and Vinod let me go.

When it's just the four of us again, Jess looks at me apologetically. Still, she can't seem to say anything. Because again, SECRETS.

I throw my hands up in surrender. If I wanted answers, I got even more questions.

Delia and I start to walk away, but Jess catches up to me,

grabbing my wrist in a loose hold. When I turn, she has actual tears in her eyes. No fake sincerity here.

"Come over tonight," she says so quietly, barely moving her lips, that I'd swear she learned somewhere how to throw her voice. She could be a ventriloquist. But that would be creepy.

I look down. "I don't know," I say, feeling the fatigue saturate my bones. All these questions, so few answers. Wouldn't it just be easier to bury my head in a pillow and sleep until morning?

But something in her wide brown eyes makes me falter, something so familiar, I feel like I can't say no.

So I say, "Maybe."

Even though what I mean is "Yes."

* * *

At home, Mom pats the frizz in her hair down.

"How do I look?" she asks, trying her best to tame the monster. At home, we joked that she had poodle hair. It's curly and sticks up at every odd angle.

"You look like a concerned citizen," I say.

The sun set an hour ago. It's just about six thirty, and Mom should be out the door. I still haven't decided whether or not it's worth it to sneak out to Jess's.

"Remember," Mom says, "doors stay locked. Anything happens, you send me one of those Chatter-whatsits."

Delia cocks her head. "Maybe we should just call you."

"What? I'm perfectly capable of figuring it out," Mom says, eyeing her phone warily. "Just don't open the door for anyone. And whatever you do, do *not* go outside."

No can do, Mom, I think.

She points to the fridge. "Sweet potato and portobello mushrooms for dinner. There are brownies for dessert. Wash your plates when you're done. With *soap*."

She's rattling off instructions like we've never been left alone before. It occurs to me that Mom is nervous. Not about leaving us, but about going to the meeting. I guess it never occurred to me that maybe Mom was afraid to make new friends, too. We've all been burned by the Dunlaps.

"The meeting goes until eight thirty, but rumor has it these things always go long, depending on how many questions there are at the end."

"'Rumor has it?'" I tease.

"Well"—Mom blushes—"the librarians were pretty chatty until I broke their photocopier."

I close the gap between Mom and me and take her by the shoulders the same way she's done to me so many times when I couldn't stop fiddling with my hair or my clothes or the strap on my backpack.

"You're gonna do great," I say, and she gives me a shaky smile, but that's all she gives me. She's still Mom. She's still tough as nails.

There's something else, though, something she's not telling us. I can't shake the feeling that there's something more to this meeting tonight than seismic talk. And no, it's not about Delia's flatulence.

"I want to hear that door lock as soon as I close it," she says. "I haven't had time to get a duplicate key made yet, so I'm leaving mine with you girls in case of emergency. But there won't be any emergency if you stick to my rules. Got it?"

She eyes us closely.

"Mom, we're fiiiiiine," Delia says, practically pushing her out the door. "Have a good night at the meeting. Learn about seismic things. Take notes. Be prepared for a two-hour presentation when you get home for your obedient, beautiful children. Byeeeeeeee!"

She locks the door as soon as she closes it on Mom, then turns around and leans on the door, sighing loudly.

"Finally!" she says. "I say we give it five minutes, then make our move to Jess's."

"Whoa, whoa," I reply, holding up my hands. "Who says we're going?"

"You did! You said we're going!" Delia says.

"Yeah, well, that was before . . ."

I've got no excuses. But I'm not sure I want to drag Delia into this mess. Besides, if Mom's going to ground me forever, why bring my little sis along, too?

And even *more* besides, what danger could I be putting Delia in by going outside?

"Before what?" she asks.

What I know for sure, though, is that if I don't take her to meet up with Jess tonight, *I'll* be the one to disappoint her. I couldn't do that to her, not after we've seen so much disappointment in our lives already. That much is certain.

I sigh. "Do we even know where Jess lives?"

Delia does a little hop and squeals, then shows me her phone screen.

"221 Dovetail Lane. Last house on the right."

It's my last chance to tell her no.

I don't. I'm a pushover.

"Get your shoes," I say. "We have one hour."

* * *

It's becoming clearer and clearer that no one goes out in Raven Brooks. Like, they go to school or go to work for a few hours . . . and then they go home. Day in, day out. School. Work. Home. School. Work. Home.

Maybe the people in this town run the odd errand to the store or the bank. Perhaps they grab a bite to eat at one of the taquerias, but they probably take it to go. I don't think I've seen a single person sitting in a café with a newspaper, or someone walking their dog. Or a single baby being strolled. Not since we moved here, anyway.

In fact, the only time I've seen a crowd bigger than ten outside of school was that first day, with the mob of people who stormed the forest looking for who knows what.

The memory casts a fresh chill down my spine, and I'm glad for my cat-ear hoodie tonight. The wind is particularly biting.

"RavenMaps says we take the next left onto Friendly Court," Delia says, the glow from her phone casting a blue light over her face. I still can't get over how few working streetlights exist in this place. Like they needed it to be any eerier than it already is.

"You know, for a knockoff app, the maps feature is actually pretty good," Delia says. "I guess that's the benefit of having a system entirely for your town?"

"Yeah, I guess," I reply.

I'm only pretending to be grumpy. It's the only way I can think of to hide the fact that I'm more than a little freaked out. When we were leaving the apartment, for just a second, I could have sworn I smelled burning. It was gone as fast as it arrived, but I haven't been able to shake the memory of what usually comes with that smell. And if anything happens to Delia . . . well, I don't want to think about that.

We're just going to a friend's house, I tell myself. *Just like kids have been doing since the beginning of time. The dinosaurs probably did it, too. The cave people probably went to each other's caves. All fine . . .*

"Aren't you even a little curious about what Jess has to say?" Delia asks. "I mean, obviously she knows that we know that she knows something. And if she knows that we know that she knows, maybe she'll, you know, help us . . . know?"

"Huh?" I ask. Okay, my superpower is good, but it's not good enough to know what Delia is trying to say.

Delia stops in her tracks. I walk ahead a few steps before I notice she's not beside me.

"It's like you don't even care that we're stuck in Bizarro Land with zero answers," Delia says, arms crossed. "Just yesterday, you were talking codes and ciphers. And now you're some kind of . . . worrywart!"

"Am not," I shoot back.

"Am too," she says.

"Ugh," I mumble.

"Look, if you want to go home, go," she says, clearly a bit angry with me. "I'll go to Jess's alone. Just because you don't care about making new friends or finding answers in this place doesn't mean *I* don't care."

"I care," I reply, in a softer voice than I meant to. "It's just . . . dangerous."

Dangerous. The word is out of my mouth before I can stop it, tumbling from my mouth like too much pepper when you flip open the wrong side.

"What's so dangerous about making friends?" she yells loudly enough for her voice to echo off the empty asphalt.

"I'm not just talking about that!"

"Then what *are* you talking about?"

"I was followed!"

Delia stops, her hands dropping from the grip they had on her hips. They hang limp at her sides now. Her face creases with worry. I regret everything.

"Like, by a person? Or—"

"I don't know," I say. "I mean, I think I was. Maybe it's nothing . . ."

But it's not nothing, and it's too late for me to hide it from Delia now. She's already seen my face.

"The other day, when I went out and you wondered where I was, there was this truck, and then I went into the woods, and—"

"You went into the woods? Like, where the crazy mob of people went into the woods? *Those* woods?"

"I didn't have a choice! The truck was following me. And anyway, there was this . . . I don't even know how to . . . like probably a man, but . . ."

"But . . . ?" Delia says, hanging on every word, even though half the words I'm saying are complete nonsense.

"A bird."

Delia's quiet for a second. She's waiting for more. There isn't more, though. That's it.

"A bird," she repeats.

"A bird," I confirm. "But like, huge. Man-sized. Maybe bigger."

Her eyes grow slowly. "Like the carving in the fence?"

I nod slowly. "I've seen it other places, too."

"That's . . . Pip, that's freaky."

"I know!"

"Why didn't you tell me?"

"Because it's freaky!"

"Yeah, but I'm your sister!"

"I didn't want to scare you!"

"You *love* to scare me!"

She has a point there.

"But this was, like . . . actual scary stuff. Like, he's sending me ChatterBack scary stuff."

"Whoa. Really?"

"Yes," I say, and it's the first time I've said it out loud. That . . . thing . . . is definitely the one sending me those messages.

We're quiet for a minute as we consider the new facts before us: Delia now knows there's more to fear than before, and I know that Delia can handle it.

I think.

When I see Delia's gaze fixed on the road ahead, I assume at first she's still contemplating what I've told her.

It's only after I follow her stare that I see the house.

At one point, it was probably beautiful. The blue paint was, I'm sure, cheery in a clear-sky kind of way. The front porch might have held rocking chairs or a game of Go Fish. The boarded-up windows could have glowed under a warm light against a scene of a family watching TV together or eating dinner. The yard—nothing but weeds and debris now—could have been serene. Maybe. At some point.

It's hard to imagine any of that now, though. And it's not because of the chipped and weather-beaten siding, or the scaffolding along the side of the house, or the broken glass framing the edges of windows blocked by plywood and plastic.

No, it's hard to see how this could have been a home instead of a hollowed-out house because of the angry black and red spray paint screaming across the front of it.

Words like "CURSED" and "OMEN" and "MURDERER" cover every available inch of space, and whatever surface has been spared by paint is splattered with rotten food or, unnervingly, burnt. The dark char marks are visible even under the meager light of the night sky.

"Um," I breathe.

"For a house on Friendly Court, it seems like no one sure wanted to be friends with *this* one," Delia says.

We move closer to the house. We have to pass it to get to

Dovetail Lane, but I don't think that's why we can't seem to stop staring at it. There's something . . . *alive* about this house. Which makes zero sense. It's obviously abandoned. There couldn't possibly be anything living in it. But it jumps out at me like a house never has before. Almost like it has a heartbeat. Almost like . . .

"Do you smell something?" Delia asks suddenly, shattering my concentration.

I take a whiff.

The smell of smoke.

I swivel and peer down the street behind us, desperately trying to parse motionless shadows from moving ones. Everything seems still. I don't see even a flicker of movement.

Until . . .

There, at the edge of the house five houses down, just beyond the tall, twisting juniper—is a thing. A *moving* thing.

It emerges slowly, like liquid oozing from a crevice, forming into a stooped figure. Gnarled shreds hang from limp limbs, its face narrowing to a curved beak.

"Delia," I whisper. "Run."

"Pip? Pip, what is that?" Delia asks frantically.

"Run."

She doesn't ask again. We take off in the direction of Dovetail Lane, the flashing raven on Delia's app pointing us in the right direction.

"Don't look back," I order Delia, and she doesn't argue.

"This way!" she says, her voice tiny and high. I can hear her breath turning to a wheeze.

Even though I said, "Don't look back," I don't follow my own advice. I chance one quick glance over my shoulder, and maybe I can still see the shadow, or maybe that's just the juniper, but as the toe of my Converse catches a divot in the road, I stumble forward. It doesn't take long, though. Maybe it's adrenaline pushing me forward. I get right back to it and continue running.

"Just one more block," Delia says after what simultaneously feels like forever and no time at all.

I'm *sure* I can still smell the burning.

"Just around this corner," she says, and like a beacon, a green street sign reading DOVETAIL LANE glows ahead.

"Hurry!" I pant, grabbing her by the hand.

Then, just as we round the corner, we hit a wall.

A wall? No, a chest. And not a treasure chest.

The chest of someone very tall.

CHAPTER 9

I'm flailing before I can even get back on my feet.

"Back away, bird creep!" I screech. (If you're going to walk the walk, you might as well talk the talk.)

"Bring it, Squatch!" shouts a voice I'm sure I recognize, but I can't be sure until I open my eyes.

I still have my hands up in something that at least resembles a defensive stance when I realize the figure is actually very familiar. It's Vinod, and he's with Jess.

Vinod is frozen in a position I can only describe as "dance-y." He has one arm bent at his side, another above his head, and a leg tucked behind him like a crane.

Not exactly the bird man I was afraid of.

I only notice Jess is standing there when she gently pushes Vinod's leg to the ground.

"Did you just call me 'bird creep'?" he asks. He has the nerve to sound offended.

"You thought I was the Skokie Sasquatch?" I muster, still searching for my lost breath.

"Look, it sounded like a herd of elephants was headed this way," Vinod replies defensively. He's trying to smooth his hair into place, but a giant chunk at the back of his head keeps springing up.

A dead leaf from a tree limb above us rattles, and something skitters down its trunk and across the yard beside us.

I spin so fast I see stars, and Delia is so close to me, we're practically sharing a kidney. At any second, the bird man will lope around the corner, dragging its shaggy feathers and hooked beak.

Run, run, little rabbit.

"Whoa, there," Jess says, her hands up. "It's a squirrel, not an axe murderer. What were you running from anyway?"

A giant bird.

A man in a truck.

A mustachioed maniac.

Name the day, and I'll name the reason I'm running.

"Just in a hurry to get here," I say, squeezing Delia's wrist so she knows to play along. I'm still not sure what is safe to share with Vinod and Jess, and frankly, I'm not super eager to give away all my secrets before hearing someone else's first. For all I know, they're making fun of me, and maybe Ally paid this whole town to play a prank on us Tillmans. Besides, Vinod and Jess promised us some answers tonight. Let's see if they keep their word.

Delia must feel the same because she doesn't argue.

Jess and Vinod exchange a cryptic look, then turn around and lead us presumably in the direction of Jess's house. Neither me nor Delia hesitates, and we follow them there.

We make a weird foursome, I'll admit it. Delia and I, three days into living in our new town, which feels like anyplace but home, wondering if the two people who've invited us to hang out tonight are actual friends or just players in some sort of elaborate trick to embarrass us.

Or worse.

And completing our foursome is Jess and Vinod, the only two people who have acknowledged any kind of oddities in this town, who I want to trust *so* desperately I'm inches away from spilling absolutely everything that's happened to us just so they can tell me what it's all about. Talk about power dynamics.

But Delia and I are completely silent as we walk, taking turns looking back to be sure we're not being followed. And Jess and Vinod keep exchanging glances that stand for words. I think if they don't start talking soon, I'm going to spontaneously combust.

How's that for seismic activity?

Delia breaks our silence as we make our way to Jess's.

"So," she says, as if tasting her own voice for the first time ever. "That house on Friendly Court. Is it for sale?"

What in the scalloped potatoes, I think. *Who in their right mind would want to move into that house? And why does Delia care?*

"Cuz, you know, our apartment's a little cramped, and I'm sure with a little paint and some new curtains, the place would only be ninety-five percent creepy. It's clocking at a solid one hundred on the haunt-o'-meter right now, but it could definitely use some TLC."

Stop it, I think. *You can't seriously be considering living . . . there.*

Jess and Vinod seem to agree with me. They swap another look.

Then Jess nods. She drops her voice real low so it's more like a whisper.

"The Peterson house," she says.

Peterson?

"Oh! Like, Theodore Peterson?" I ask, and Jess stops walking. Huh. I've managed to surprise her.

"Yes," she says, but somehow makes it sound like a question, lifting an eyebrow at me.

I'm keeping this part secret, though. I don't want to give too much away about Cousin Marcia and what she left for us. It's better that Jess doesn't know how we know about Theodore Peterson.

"It was his parents' house first, I heard," says Vinod, apparently a little more willing to spill the beans than Jess or me. "They were some kind of scientists or meteorologists or something. I guess they don't matter too much—that part's a little murky anyway."

"Ah, yes," Delia says. "Murky. How unusual for Raven Brooks."

"Okay," I cut in. "So, some guy inherited that house. And?"

I decide to see how much they'll fill me in. What they leave out could be more telling than what they actually say. I read about this in a *Learn to Tell the Future* book I bought at a school book fair at home. I wonder if Raven Brooks even has school book fairs.

"Peterson was one of those big brains, you know?" says Vinod. "The kind that can, like, invent a telescope from a cheese grater. He probably could have been a Da Vinci type."

"Could have been . . ." I repeat.

Surprisingly, it's Jess who picks up the story.

"Some people think there's a thin line between genius and, you know . . ."

Bird? I think. Not sure I've heard that one before.

"Anyway, some mega-super-rich people who basically built the town—" Vinod continues.

"The Tavishes," Jess interjects.

"Right, the Tavishes owned the Golden Apple Corporation, which was basically a fancy candy factory. But apparently it was really good. My mom says the Golden Apples were life-altering. Like, I don't think she's known happiness since she last tasted one of those things. Not even when I was born. And I'm not even mad about it. I just wanna taste one, just once in my life."

A strange left turn in the conversation, I'll admit. But I feel for Vinod. We went without the fruit leather for three days, and it was painful.

"You'll need to learn how to bend time, then," Jess says. "They went belly-up the minute the amusement park flopped."

"I'm not sure I'd call that a 'flop,'" Vinod says. "More like a crash and burn. Emphasis on the 'burn.'"

"Yeah, burn for sure," Jess agrees.

I guess this is more info than we had before?

"Why, though?" I ask, pretending I didn't just read about the Golden Apple Amusement Park misfortune. "Why would that bankrupt an entire empire?"

Another look from Jess and Vinod.

"Well . . ." Jess trails off.

"That's where things get a little murky," Vinod adds.

Hmm. I read Mom's newspaper articles. I thought it was pretty straightforward. Amusement parks aren't supposed to kill kids. They're, like, supposed to do the opposite—make kids feel *alive*, so much that they'll keep dishing out for expensive tickets and having all their important birthdays and memories there. One little girl's death should have been reason enough to close anyplace, *especially* an amusement park.

"Peterson's name was all over that park," Vinod adds. "He designed it. They flew him in from Germany or France or something to do it. He was a big deal, and the Golden Apple people wanted everyone to know they got this amazing, smart dude to build the most epic rides anyone had ever seen. But then something happened and . . ."

"Peterson kinda went off the rails after that," Jess finishes.

"Well, from what I've heard, I'm not sure he wasn't totally on the rails *before* it," says Vinod.

Delia's caught on to what Vinod left off.

"Off the rails how?" she asks.

Vinod drops his voice real low and takes another look around before practically mouthing back.

"Like stashing-his-own-kids-away-in-his-basement off the rails," he whispers.

What? I've heard of creepy, but this . . . is *beyond* creepy. Mega creepy. Stuff-from-nightmares creepy. I already knew things were pretty grim with the poor girl from the Rotten Core, but I assumed that was some kind of tragedy, like a car accident. Horrible, but not really anyone's fault—most of the time.

This? I'm not sure how much more macabre this story can get.

"At least one of his kids didn't make it out alive," Jess says so quietly, I'm not sure I hear her right at first.

But when I hear Delia suck in her breath, I know my hearing can't be too far off.

"What do you mean, *at least* one of them?" I say. "How many were there? How did they die? How hard can that be to confirm?" I feel like I have five hundred more questions than when I started, and honestly, I haven't gotten any satisfying answers.

Neither of them says anything. They've picked a pretty frustrating time to stop talking.

"Ugh!" I groan, my voice doing that frantic high-pitched thing Mom's does when she gets nervous.

"Nobody's keeping it from you," Jess says. "Believe it or not, there are things we don't know, either."

Huh. I guess I hadn't realized that. Maybe Jess and Vinod really don't know. Maybe we're more alike than I thought.

Jess continues walking in silence. When Delia and I slow down, Vinod keeps pace with us.

"Jess has . . . a lot going on," he says, his attempt at

apologizing for Jess. I'm the one who should be apologizing, though. All this time, I've been assuming my family's the only one completely in the dark.

Maybe Raven Brooks is keeping secrets from more people than just us.

Or maybe Jess and Vinod are as . . . interesting . . . as the rest of Raven Brooks.

"It's, ah . . . Vinod, nothing here makes sense. I mean *nothing*."

I step closer, so I'm just inches from his face, and he looks like he wants to take a step back, but he stands where he is.

"It's not November. It's July," I say firmly.

At first, I think Vinod is going to cry. He doesn't really know how to react, and I realize I don't know how to react, either. I mean, this is all too absurd, right? How can a whole town think it's November? It's July—and also, why is this calendar fluke somehow the *least* unusual thing about Raven Brooks?

Then, without moving a single muscle around his mouth, Vinod whispers, "Don't say anything else until we get inside." His eyes are so wide and for a moment, I wonder if he's possessed.

Then, he releases the hold on his face and looks around like he's trying to see if anyone heard him.

"C'mon, we're almost there," he says, his voice as casual as if we were on our way to a baseball game with some friends. "Man, I am *hu-uh-ngry*!"

Delia and I exchange looks, because now that we've made it this far, what else is there to but follow the weird?

We catch up to Jess just as we're rounding the corner onto Dovetail Lane. I can't help it. I let out an audible gasp.

There, not ten feet from my right side, is the tree line we first followed upon driving through the culvert and collapsing the wall behind us. Rising from the trees like a vine-choked weed is the giant billboard asking where these missing souls have gone. The same trees through which the angry mob had filtered that very first afternoon we rolled into our new town now sway and snap in the inexplicable autumn breeze, the spaces between them pitch-black and cavernous.

And there, directly across the street with yellow light pouring from the downstairs windows, is the pink house where the lady with the brown eyes beckoned us, the house from which we were trapped in the garage, where Delia took a granola bar, where we escaped without a word.

Jess's house—221 Dovetail Lane—is the house with the garage.

And we're walking right back into it.

CHAPTER 10

"What?" asks Jess. She's noticed Delia and me staring.

Delia, normally the world's biggest truth-saying chatterbox, has got nothing.

"Uh," she manages.

"What?" Jess asks again.

It's up to me.

"I think we've met your mom before," I say.

And then Jess does the strangest thing. She *laughs*.

"Pretty unlikely," she says. "Because *I've* never even met her. She died when I was a baby."

Then she turns and starts up the winding walkway toward the front door of the pink house.

I feel like a total jerk (after all, there's no reason that woman in the garage couldn't have been Jess's aunt or a guardian or a foster parent). Mom was adopted, too. I should have known better.

Vinod catches up to us.

"Look, I know you're super confused," he whispers.

"You could say that, yeah," I say, glad he's at least acknowledging it.

"You just need to trust us. Do you think you can do that?"

I want to believe Vinod. On this dark street with his wide-open eyes, there's sincerity on his face. Pure and simple.

But I can't bring myself to say yes. I have no idea what I'm involved in.

I do follow him, though, and Delia trails close behind.

When we step through Jess's door, I can smell beans stewing on the stovetop, with a big ol' bay leaf in the middle.

Vinod rushes past us. "Please tell me your aunt made dinner. I am so hungry."

"You ate a granola bar half an hour ago, but yes, my aunt made dinner," Jess says.

"I . . . I think I might cry," says Vinod, and he's not even pretending to be dramatic. There's a little tear pooling in his eye.

"Your love for food is outrageous," Jess says, shaking her head.

I hear Delia's stomach grumble from where I stand.

"C'mon." Jess beckons us toward the kitchen.

As soon as we round the corner, I see a well-worn table set for five. That gives me some pause, even though this is the homiest I've felt in a while. We were expected.

"Finally," says a woman at the stove whose back is to us. "Did you take the long way or something?"

"We had a close call with a Sasquatch," Jess replies, winking at Vinod.

"Ms. Esposito, help me out here," Vinod pleads with the woman. "You've heard of the Skokie Sasquatch, haven't you?"

"Vinod, if I've learned nothing else over my lifetime, it's to believe in *absolutely everything*," says the woman, her voice raspy and fatigued, like believing *is* exhausting. "And I've told you a million times to call me Mari, or Aunt Mari like Jess and Jordy do, or call me Cleopatra for all I care. Just not Ms. Esposito. We're past that, I think."

"Okeydoke, Ms. Esposito," Vinod says, and winks at me. This must be a running gag. He drops his voice low and whispers to me, "She kept her original last name and it's just so fun to say."

When the woman—Mari—turns, she's wearing a navy pullover sweater and cuffed jeans, her long, straight brown hair done up in the same intricate braids as Jess's. She wears stacks of silver bracelets and chunky silver earrings, a silver chain around her neck tucked under her sweater's collar, and she has the same enormous brown eyes as Jess.

"Sit," Mari says, shooing us all toward the table like Delia and I have known her long enough to be "past that," too.

Three small steaming tortillas are placed on my plate, then Delia's.

"Guests first. No offense, Vinod," says Aunt Mari.

"Just as long as I'm fed," he says, looking a little grumpy.

Mom's not a half-bad cook, but this is something *extra* amazing. The smell is everywhere, and if Raven Brooks were cloaked in tortillas and Sazón instead of smoke, it would almost certainly be more tolerable. I immediately take a big helping of the jackfruit and beans and wrap them in the tortillas with a bit more hot sauce.

Aunt Mari returns to the stove and pulls out a small glass dish. She spatulas them onto a plate and sets it in front of Vinod, whose eyes go round, like moons.

"Vegan enchiladas."

Vinod's smile is wide.

The tacos are even better than they smell, and suddenly, this house with the garage doesn't seem nearly as terrifying.

"I'm sorry about—uh, our first day," I say, licking some salsa off my index finger. "It was a really long drive and we were overwhelmed and Mom—"

"You don't have to explain anything," Mari says. Then she grabs a wad of paper towels and places them on the table, as normal as can be. "And by the way, it's not November."

Delia drops her whole taco. Thankfully, it falls onto her plate. I almost do the same.

"*You* know it's not November; *we* know it's not November, and yet—"

She waits.

It's a puzzle. A cipher.

"But nobody else does," I finish for her, and she nods.

"We're pretty sure it's July twenty-fifth, give or take a day. I forgot to keep count once, and now I'm all off," says Vinod.

"Twenty-sixth," Delia corrects him, and I'm surprised to realize she's been keeping count, too. I certainly hadn't. I guess she wanted to hold on to whatever thread of truth she thought was left.

"So," I say, suddenly no longer hungry. "Is this whole town, what, bewitched by a wizard? Blessed by the Thanksgiving Fairy? What, it's just always the same day here?" I sound like Delia.

"Er," says Jess, putting her elbows on the table so she can

cradle her chin in her hands. "Time just sort of . . . keeps resetting itself."

"Or *someone* keeps resetting it," says Mari, her eyebrow lifting the way I've seen Jess's arch before.

"That's . . ." I say, "possible? Someone in this town is just resetting the clock, like skipping ahead on a video game console?"

Jess nods. "Welcome to Raven Brooks. Where the wildest impossibilities come true."

"So what, every week the clock just starts over?" I ask.

"Not every week," says Vinod.

"Sometimes it takes a week. Sometimes less. Once we got all the way to November twenty-first," says Jess.

"I thought I was finally gonna have Thanksgiving dinner," mopes Vinod.

"Vinod's dad does this whole feast," Jess explains, looking downright wistful. "It's beyond amazing."

"And then someone hits the rewind button, and you're where you started?" Delia asks, bringing us back to the topic.

"More like the reset button," says Mari. "No matter what, we always come back to November second."

"Reset Day," Jess says gloomily.

Delia and I look at each other.

"I know you don't believe us," Vinod adds. "If I were you, I probably wouldn't believe us, either."

But that's not it. Somehow, this explanation makes sense. I mean,

scientifically, it makes as much sense as my science-fair volcano when I was seven, which was supposed to explode with lava but instead fell apart on the way to school, but this . . . answer . . . kind of answers, everything. Somehow.

"It's not that. We *do* believe you," I say, surprising myself. "I actually can't believe how much we believe you. It's just that . . ."

In a way, it's easier to believe the unbelievable than to pretend to believe the lie everyone else seems to be living.

"Our dad . . ." Delia starts, and her voice falters.

"He died on November first," I say.

Mari, Jess, and Vinod are all quiet. Vinod drops his gaze to the table. So does Jess, but Mari casts a worried glance toward Jess. She reaches for Jess's hand and clasps it. Then Jess speaks.

"I'm sorry about your dad," Jess says. "My dad . . . we can't find him, either. He went missing."

That's all she can manage before she starts to cry. She wipes the tears away angrily, leaving red streaks on her face.

"He is my brother, Enzo," Mari says softly as she pulls Jess closer, stroking her hair. "We've lived in Raven Brooks our whole lives, and it's definitely a town full of oddities. This one has me really perplexed, though. I'm looking after Jess and Jordy until we find him."

Enzo. That must be Enzo Esposito, the man in the grocery store newspaper. The man on the billboard with the salt-and-pepper goatee.

"Hang on," Delia says. "The newspaper . . . didn't it say your dad went missing November first?"

I was just thinking the same thing. It feels like more than a horrible coincidence that he disappeared the same day Dad died. The day before time started resetting in this town.

"You said before that you think someone might be doing this? The resetting, I mean."

Mari nods, releasing Jess from her hold. "It's just a theory," she says.

"It's a pretty good theory," Vinod adds. "I mean, I know I'm the resident conspiracy enthusiast and all, but—"

"It's Peterson," Jess says all of a sudden. It's so matter-of-fact, I don't doubt her for a second.

But why?

"Peterson, the park guy?" I ask. "I thought he was long gone."

"Please tell me he's not still living in that house," Delia says.

"I don't know," says Jess, "but Dad thought he was the one behind it, and he's got personal experience." She motions to her aunt. "They both do."

Mari, strangely, looks less convinced. "It's . . ." She squirms a little. I can tell she's struggling. "It's complicated."

Jess is adamant, though. "But it isn't complicated at all. We find Peterson, we find my dad."

"Has anyone ever searched the house? I mean, Peterson's house?" I venture, hating the thought of being the one to suggest going anywhere near the place with its boarded-up windows and rotting porch.

"Absolutely not," Mari says, cutting Jess off before she can share her thoughts. "Saying that place is unsafe is the understatement of the century."

"But—" Jess protests.

"And your dad knew that, too, which is why he never would have set a *toe* in there. Forget about it. We're staying as far away from that house as possible. Final answer."

There's something in Mari's voice that makes me uncomfortable. It's like the first time I ever got into real trouble with my mom. I'd wandered off in a sporting goods store without telling her. I didn't mean to, but the tennis balls were calling, and before I knew it, Mom was nowhere in sight, and I was surrounded by the legs of strangers. When my mom and I were finally reunited by a store clerk—after what felt like a hundred years—I was terrified. That fear was nothing compared to what I felt after Mom was done with me, though. It wasn't that she took away my beloved Mr. Badger for a week, or that she told my dad later that evening, or even that I never looked at a tennis ball the same way after that.

It was the fact that Mom was scared. Hands-shaking, voice-cracking, silent-treatment-for-the-rest-of-the-day scared. The only thing she said to me that entire day was "I thought I'd never see you again." That was it. That was enough for me to know that grown-ups get scared, so scared that they don't know what to do, and that was the first moment I ever realized that I wouldn't always be safe.

That's how it sounds when Mari says we're not to go near the Peterson house.

Vinod sneaks back into the conversation. "Aunt Mari has a different theory."

"Hang on, hang on," I say, the questions in my brain fighting over which gets to come out first. It's been getting pretty crowded up there the past few days. "How is it that time is resetting for everyone else, but not you three?"

Vinod's lanky arms spread wide. "Three? Well, now there's six! Welcome to the club nobody wants to join!"

"We have no idea why we were marked 'safe' from Reset Day. We tried getting help, but there was no way to reach the outside world. Until you came to town, we thought we were the only ones."

I nod. It's no small feat to get into Raven Brooks these days.

"Yeah, the wall," I say. "Speaking of. What's up with the wall? Has it always been there? Was it meant to keep us out—or keep everyone *in*?"

"Ding, ding, ding! More hot-ticket questions to add to the never-ending pile of *who-the-heck-knows*," says Vinod, and with sarcasm that lights up his whole face, adds, "Isn't this the most fun game ever?"

"Hmm," Mari says. "But if you're here, I think time kept going for Marcia Tillman, too. She never told us."

Jess barks a single laugh. "Like she would have."

Mari thumps Jess's shoulder with the back of her hand, then apologizes to us. "I'm sorry for your loss," she says.

"Thank you. But we didn't know her."

"Really? And she left you everything in her will?" asks Jess. "I thought maybe you guys or Marcia had some more answers for us. But this is just more questions."

"I still don't get it," pipes in Delia, who I realize now has been way quieter than probably ever in her entire life.

"Which part?" asks Vinod. "There's a lot to choose from."

"Why is Reset Day such a secret from everyone else? What if you just told people what was happening?"

Jess's tone softens. "Would you believe *us* if we told *you*? I mean, you know because out there"—she gestures wide, I guess pointing to places beyond Raven Brooks—"the world is doing its thing. Time is passing."

"But in here," says Vinod, "nobody thinks any different."

"We think that whoever it is, they know who we are. They have more intel on us than we do about them."

Delia gasps. "Ohmygosh," she says in one word. "We found a camera in our apartment."

Mari leans forward over the table. "Really?" she asks. "Was it on? Did it have any labels? Anything you remember?"

"I don't know if it was on, but I think so. No labels. Our Mom found it while we were at school. It's a spy cam for sure."

"You need to search the rest of your place. Search it more than once. The store, too. If they were watching your cousin Marcia, they're probably watching you, too." Mari bites her lip.

"Which is why you don't talk about any of this except for—"

"Except for places we know are safe," says Vinod.

"Also," Jess says, "we're kind of trying to keep a low profile. For a few reasons."

"Okaaaay?" I say, for the first time tonight not sure if I want answers.

Jess doesn't give me a choice, though. It seems they're just as eager to spill as I've been to ask.

"Dad's wanted by the police," she says.

"That's a little extreme," Mari corrects. "My brother isn't a wanted man by any stretch. But the PD is interested in talking to him."

"He didn't do anything," Jess rushes to clarify.

"Well, technically, but—" says Mari.

"He probably broke some stupid Raven Brooks rule—"

"It's called the law," says Mari.

"It's called stupid," Jess argues.

"What did he do?" I interrupt. Seriously. Do these people know they can, you know, not be cryptic?

"He signed in a visitor during the seismic testing period," says Jess after a long pause, a confession that hardly seems worth confessing. Still, no one says anything after that.

"I don't get it," I say for what feels like the millionth time tonight.

"Um, you might have figured this out already, but Raven Brooks is a little . . . shy?" Vinod tries.

"We don't like outsiders," Jess corrects.

"You don't say," I add. It's my turn to get snarky. Our welcome here has been anything but warm, straight down to the weather.

And speaking of the weather.

"What is with this seismic testing?" I ask, setting aside the whole not-nice-to-strangers thing for a second.

Mari sighs. "The weather here is unusual. It has been ever since I was your age. That's not really the point, though. The point is, Enzo signed someone in during the restricted period, and because it happened right before he disappeared, the police have questions. They want to know what he was doing and, more importantly, why."

"And every time the day resets, they start looking for him all over again," says Vinod.

"Hang on, if time keeps resetting, then the police don't know how long he's actually been missing."

"Exactly," says Mari.

"And every time it resets, the investigation starts all over again. From the beginning," I say. I'm beginning to catch on. This whole town is one absurd time loop. It's not time travel— time-travel rules never really make sense, but it's some kind of supernatural doing. Or some super-genius doing.

Huh. A super-genius kind of like how they described . . . that Peterson guy.

Delia's back to her usual self, practically jumping off the table.

"Why did you hide us in the garage?" she asks Mari. "And what were all those people going into the forest for?"

Mari's whole face softens when she looks back at Delia. My sister has a way of doing that to people.

"I didn't mean to scare you," Mari replies. "But the day you arrived, time reset. For everyone else, it was the first day Enzo went missing. Strangers showing up on the day one of Raven Brooks's people went missing would've been cause for question.

So, number one, hiding you was for safety. Number two, we were going into the woods to find him. This is how it always starts. It's before the police discover he signed in a guest. It's before people start to suspect him."

"We had no idea who you were," adds Jess. "And to be honest, we were a bit afraid of you, too. Technically, you shouldn't have even been able to get past the wall. That's why we didn't invite you inside. Garage only, Aunt Mari's rules."

"We couldn't have known you were moving to town," says Mari apologetically.

"No offense, but we had other things to worry about than who inherited Marcia Tillman's store," Jess adds.

"Marcia was . . . kind of an oddball," says Vinod, then immediately looks down sheepishly. "Sorry. She just wasn't exactly a town favorite."

I stifle a laugh. "I mean, I've gathered as much," I say. "But if she was working on something, I have no idea what it was. And neither does my sister. Or my mom, for that matter." I don't tell them about Mom's trip to the library. I trust Mari, Jess, and Vinod, probably more than I should, but it's not my intel to share.

Rap! Rap! Rap! There's three hard knocks at the door.

I snap to attention, and I spot Mari grip the table edge.

"Did you invite anyone else over?" she hisses to Jess.

"Of course not!" Jess replies a little too sharply. I guess that's what the paranoia will do to you.

The rest of us shake our heads. Not it.

The rapping starts again, this time louder.

"Open up! Raven Brooks PD!"

Mari's eyes get as round as saucers.

"Okay. Act natural," she says through gritted teeth, then slowly rises to answer the door. "And, you two?" She points at me and Delia.

Delia and I clasp hands.

"Hide!"

Delia and I immediately scramble to find someplace safe. But we don't get the opportunity. No sooner do we hear the door open and Aunt Mari greet the officers with feigned confusion than they tromp right through the door. I'm betting they didn't even wipe their feet first, which—honestly?—is just plain rude.

"Step aside, Maritza. We need to speak with your brother."

"Enzo isn't here," Aunt Mari protests. "You know that!"

"Oooh, I smell jackfruit."

"Focus, Darryl!"

"Sorry."

As I'm scrambling to find the most epic "hide" place in the strangest game of hide-and-seek probably ever, I run straight into the chest of someone taller than me. This time, he's wearing a dark brown uniform and looks as startled to see me as I am to be buried nose-first between his badge and his shirt pocket.

"Who are you?" demands the woman in uniform beside him. I never knew that particular question could sound so accusatory. I bite my tongue hard so I don't retort the way I imagine Mom responding.

"Nobody important. We were just leaving," Delia replies. She tries to sidle past the woman, but the woman holds her hand out, barring us from passing. She has thick thighs and a stomach so flat, she probably does fifty thousand crunches a day. If I weren't scared, I'd be impressed by her workout routine.

"What's your name, young lady?"

"D-Delia," she stammers, and I instinctively step in front of her. I don't care if you're wearing a uniform or you can crush golden apples with your abs, nobody intimidates my sister.

"She's *eleven*," I say, staring the officer straight in the eyes. Well, I try to stare her straight in the eyes. She's wearing sunglasses. At night. Inside.

"Write that down, Darryl," she says to the officer next to her, who is staring longingly at our jackfruit remnants on the table. "Delia, age eleven."

"Eve, what's this all abou—"

"*Officer* Ruston," the officer cuts Aunt Mari off, whipping around so fast, her blond ponytail actually makes a thwapping sound.

Aunt Mari is clearly very tense.

"Officer, what can I do for you? These kids are just friends of the family. They go to Raven Brooks Middle."

"I've never seen them before," says Officer Eve.

"Of course you have," says Mari smoothly.

Vinod joins in the act seamlessly. "You know, Delia and Piper Tillman. Marcia Tillman's cousins."

Officer Eve eyes me closely through her glasses.

147

"Hmm," she says, squinting so hard I'm not sure she can see through all that sunglasses tint. "Your hands do kind of look like Marcia's."

What is it with these people and hands?!

"It's awfully coincidental that you two showed up now of all times. Are you aware that we're looking for a mystery guest signed into town by Ms. Esposito's brother, Enzo? During the restricted period," Officer Eve says slowly, like she's chewing on the words.

I play dumb.

"No," I reply in the sweetest voice I can muster. "We're just mourning our cousin. I'm really sad."

Delia, from behind me, begins to emit alligator sobs. I make a mental note that if we ever get out of Raven Brooks alive, Mom *has* to sign her up for acting classes. This girl's got pipes.

"Hey, Mari, I don't suppose you have any extra tacos—" Officer Darryl starts.

"Darryl!" snaps Officer Eve. Ruston. Whatever.

Darryl looks like he wishes he had a tail to tuck between his legs.

"You can have the rest of mine!" Delia says to Officer Darryl, patting her fake tears on the back of her hand. I want to scoop my sister up and hug her because I cannot believe that this *works*.

"Really, you wouldn't mind—" he whispers to Delia.

"Just a minute, Miss—" Officer Eve Ruston says. She reaches for Delia's wrist. Her teeny, tiny, miniature wrist that could snap in half between Officer Eve's muscly hands. I never knew hands could be muscly. That's when I see flaming hot red.

"Get your hands off my sister!" I shout, and Officer Eve actually startles back.

"Girls," Aunt Mari hisses, but it's too late.

Officer Eve motions behind her, and I swear she's going for her handcuffs, but something rabid and wild has awakened inside of me, and I think maybe my teeth, which Ally used to tell me were too big for my face, can puncture a tiny bit of the officer's muscly hand.

I'm still seeing red when the ground beneath us starts to sway.

I'd always heard that earthquakes don't feel like shaking. They feel like sliding. Like the ground underneath the ground is slipping around on ice.

Apparently, that isn't too far off.

"Get in a doorway!" Mari shouts, raising her voice above the clamber of pots and dishes in the kitchen.

The feeling of disorientation is surreal. I was never really a fan of ice-skating. I remember how out of control I felt on the rink, my feet wobbling and buckling in all the wrong directions. That's how I feel now, and if not for the sheer terror driving me toward the doorway with Mari and Delia, I think I'd probably be standing in the middle of the kitchen, staring dumbly at the swaying pans hanging from Aunt Mari's pot rack while the rest of the world shimmies to pieces.

"This way!" shouts Jess, and she and Vinod guide Officers Eve and Darryl to the next nearest doorway around the corner.

It's only when Mari turns to me that I realize, while the earthquake was a coincidence, this was completely intentional guidance—to get the police officers out of sight.

Go! Mari mouths to me once Jess and Vinod have disappeared with them.

"What?" I nearly bark.

"Hurry, before the shaking stops!"

"But—"

"Now," Mari says in a tone that means she's *serious.*

I grab Delia.

"Piper, I'm scared," Delia croaks out.

"Shhh," I hush her, and I hold her as close as I possibly can while we bump against the walls like pinballs and grapple our way toward the door. I can't see Jess and Vinod. I can't see Officer Eve Ruston and Officer Darryl Whatever-His-Last-Name-Is. When we leave the kitchen doorway and feel the handle of the front door, I can't even see Mari anymore.

All I can see is a slanting, sliding Dovetail Lane as I fling the door open and hang on for dear life to the doorframe and we escape.

CHAPTER 11

Delia runs in the direction of Friendly Court.

"Not that way!" I shout over the rumbling, pulling her by her arm.

"We don't know any other way!" she objects, but I'm older, so she has to abide by my rules.

The ground finally stops shifting, and I think the shaking is done, at least for now. But I don't want to be anywhere near Friendly Court after what Mari and Jess and Vinod told us, and I certainly don't want to be anywhere near Jess's house now that the shaking has stopped or near the officers who clearly spell doom.

We've made it a few minutes in the opposite direction when Delia can't hold it in anymore. "Can we stop running yet?" she pants.

Ah. She thinks I have a plan.

I guess I have to pretend to have one.

"Let's just get around this corner first," I say. "At least that will put us out of sight of the house if the cops come out."

I don't even want to think about what's going to happen to Mari now that she's let us get away.

As we turn the corner, Delia bends at her waist, putting her hands on her knees.

"If I'd known I was going to do so much running tonight, I'd have worn better shoes."

"I would have not come," I say, though that's not true at all. We did get some answers, even if I didn't like them.

"I think the shaking has stopped," Delia says, and I pull out my phone. But when I try to pull up the map feature, I get nothing.

My stomach drops.

"Does yours say 'No Service,' too?" I ask.

She shakes her head. "Network must be down because of the, er . . . 'seismic activity.'" She makes air quotes around the phrase "seismic activity."

"I don't know, but I'd really like to get home in case it starts up again," I say.

Or before the police come looking to finish the interrogation they started. Or before Mom comes home to find us missing. Mom—yikes. What time is it, anyway? We're probably close to our hour up, if not already passed it.

Delia's reading my mind because she looks as panicked as I'm beginning to feel.

"I don't know the way from here," she says.

I pause to take a breath. I don't know the way, either. See also: We haven't even been in this town a week!

As though summoned, suddenly we hear a car engine advancing.

"Is that coming toward us?" I ask.

It's growing closer, wherever it's coming from.

"Yes," Delia replies in a panic. "Behind here, quick!" We duck into a carefully manicured topiary in the yard beside us.

The sound of squealing breaks emerges, then the familiar sound of a squeaking car window rolling down.

Oh no. I know that squeak.

Mom.

Mom doesn't take a second to spot our heads popping out from the topiary. She hunkers down from the car and waves a finger at us both, like we're two very disobedient dogs.

"So."

That's the only word she says. And yet, it's enough to frighten me to pieces.

Delia and I scramble into the car, and Mom floors it, her tires screeching just as we click our seat belts.

For most of the drive, Mom is silent. Which is arguably worse than if she says anything, as any kid knows. You're just left to this awful silence, and you aren't really sure if they're going to yell, or guilt-trip you, or what.

I have to break the silence.

"Mom, I'm so sorry, but—"

"But nothing," she snaps.

Another silence. This time, neither me nor Delia breaks it. But Mom does.

"Here's what I *don't* want to hear. I don't want to hear that you didn't mean to scare me, that it wasn't a big deal, that you had your phones on the entire time, that you didn't go far, or that you just *had* to go."

Hmmm. She's not leaving me with very many options for excuses.

"Do you have any idea what it feels like to wonder if you'll ever see your children again?"

"Mom, I can explain—"

"No, I don't think so." Mom's shrill voice ricochets around the car. "You were just doing what you wanted instead of what *I specifically told you to do*. Which, Delia, remind me, what was that?"

Delia makes a face. "Stay home."

"Stay home," Mom repeats. "Stay home. And you two went off, and—and—"

"Visiting Jess," Delia says.

Mom acts like Jess is some kind of monster from the deep lagoon.

"Jess."

"She's the niece of the lady with the garage. The one we hid in." As if Mom needs more of an explanation than *the lady with the garage.*

Mom slams on the break in the middle of the empty street. More silence. Then:

"I'm sorry, but you're going to have to say that again. I couldn't have possibly heard that correctly."

"Er," I reply.

"Mom, we have to tell you—" Delia tries.

"You can tell me once we've gotten out of this place," Mom says, eyes fixed on the road. It's the first time I realize we probably should have arrived home by now. Jess's house isn't this far away from the apartment. I repeat Mom's words in my head a few times before I realize what she's saying.

"Gotten out? Like, leaving?" I ask.

Mom doesn't answer. She keeps her focus on the road, her hands still fastened to the steering wheel.

"I thought we couldn't leave," says Delia. "I thought there wasn't a way out."

I stare at the side of Mom's face. She chances a quick glance at me from her mirror before retraining her eyes on the road. But in that flicker, I see fear. Whatever she learned at that meeting tonight, it was enough to make her change her mind about trying to make it work here.

"I don't understand," says Delia. "How are we even going to get out?"

"There's a part of the wall that's weakened," says Mom. "They're fixing it tomorrow, which means if we don't get out tonight . . ."

We're all quiet for a second while Mom drives.

"Was that an earthquake?" I ask. We never had earthquakes back at home.

Mom shakes her head slowly without looking at me. "I have no idea what that was. What I do know is that the meeting got cut short, and . . ." She trails off.

"And?" I say, hating every single way my brain wants to end that sentence.

"Some people . . . dressed all in black, with black hats . . ." Mom looks at me like it's too late. She has to finish. "They followed me into the parking lot. They started asking so many questions. Personal questions. I . . ."

And she was scared. Whoever these people were, they were probably zeroing in on her the way the officers were zeroing in on Delia and me. And poor Mom didn't even have tacos to distract them.

But these people were different. If they'd been police, she would have said so.

Mom shakes off the memory of the people in the black hats. I wish I could, too. Instead, I'm now stuck with the image I've conjured of them. In my mind's eye, they have suits made of shiny black feathers.

"There's a hole in the wall," says Mom, "Just beyond the grounds of the old amusement park, at the back of what used to be the parking lot. If we can get through there, we can get back to the road."

The road to *where* is the question. After tonight, anyplace feels safer than here.

Still, I haven't got the slightest idea of what might wait for us

out in the open. If no one has been able to come and go from Raven Brooks for months, how can we know if time will keep moving forward once we leave? Will we pick up where we left off? Will time return to normal? Or will these starts and stops and restarts follow us out of Raven Brooks like some sort of hive of bees?

So, because I don't know how to answer her, I say the only thing I can think of. "We'll be safe."

But I don't believe that's true any more than I believe that time will continue the way it's supposed to. I just don't know. All the rules have been broken. Every last one.

When Mom slows to a stop, it isn't at a light or a sign or even a turn. From what I can tell, it's just the middle of the road with a long stretch of more road in front, and my least favorite sight of all: a wall of trees to our left.

"There's supposed to be a road through here somewhere," Mom says through gritted teeth.

"Through the woods? Mom, no," I reply.

"It's not like I *want* to go through there!" Mom says.

"But how do you know it'll even work?" I ask.

Mom doesn't answer.

Instead, we do a slow roll up and down the empty street beside the tree line twice before locating a small opening barely big enough to fit the car.

"This feels like a terrible idea," I say, and Mom casts a warning look in my direction.

I get a horrible case of déjà vu as we crunch along the path that's barely a road and flinch as every low branch in the forest drags along the top of our car. It feels like an eternity ago that we first heard the same foreboding sound of something scraping the roof of our car.

I mean, time has no meaning anymore, so for all I know, it *was* an eternity ago.

"It should be just up the way a bit," Mom says, using her high beams to see the barely-there road.

Then, in a literal *flash*, a competing light switches on, blinding us for a second and making Mom slam on the brakes. Just ahead, high atop a mound of dirt and in the shadow of what looks to be construction trucks and lights strung up around a work site, stand at least five people, all circled around something at the top of the hill.

What that something is, I couldn't begin to guess.

What I do know is that they are there, which is right where we need to be.

"You've got to be kidding me," Mom whispers to herself. "That's where the emergency was?"

I look at her, and I guess she decides at least one thing tonight is worth explaining.

"When the shaking started, the security guard at the meeting got a call on his radio. Something about a missing construction worker. That's all I heard," she says, lowering her head to the steering wheel in defeat. "Just our luck that it's exactly where we need to pass to get out of here."

"We can get around them by going that way," Delia suggests. She points to an impossibly narrow path.

"Is that even a road?" Mom asks, peering into the dark.

"Is any of this?" counters Delia.

"Good point."

Mom really must be desperate because she slowly turns the wheel and gradually releases her foot from the brake, heading down Delia's path. She reaches to the side and cuts the headlights off to hide us further in the night's darkness.

Whatever she heard at that meeting, it scared her enough to risk everything. And here I thought Delia and I were going to win the scariest-news-of-the-night game.

"Piper. Tell me if I'm about to hit a tree," Mom says, taking in a deep breath that I don't hear her let out.

"You're always about to hit a tree in here," I say.

Why is being the cautious one always the hardest work?

We inch down the path, stopping every few seconds to make sure we aren't being followed. At any moment, I expect one of the people at the construction site to come tumbling down the hill, chasing after us for . . . I don't even know what anymore. Trespassing? The crime of being new in town? Having something to do with Jess's dad because we *dared* step foot in this super-creepy town?

"You're good," Delia says at the latest stop. "No trees. Keep going."

At last, we reach a small break in the forest. I almost feel relief. *Almost.* Then I see a different sort of wall in front of us—a brick one.

"There's no opening," Mom observes, starting to panic.

"There," I say, spotting it first.

The opening is so far down the wall, it practically disappears into the shadow of the trees.

Sure enough, there's a low ridge of brush, and just beyond, a low pile of crumbled brick. The opening in the wall is barely the width of the car. Mom's going to have to angle the car just right to get it through.

She reverses as far as she can go, the bumper dipping into the divot of a tree root.

"I'm going to have to get up enough speed to get over the bricks," she says.

"Can the tires handle that?" I ask.

"If I go too slowly, it's going to make more noise," she says, and I glance back at the harsh light of the spots still illuminating the workers. There seem to be more of them now. Commotion on top of the nearby hill is growing. People are scrambling up and down the mound, and I can hear shouting back and forth.

That's not what makes my stomach sink lower, though. It's the glare off a familiar pair of aviator glasses from the thick of the crowd. That can only mean one thing. The police have made their way to the construction site.

"Deep breath," Mom says quietly, and I can hear her pull in a giant exhale.

She'll have one shot at this, maybe two. After that, odds are either the tires will pop or the people on the hill will see us. Honestly, I'm not sure which is worse.

"Three . . ."

In just a few seconds, Raven Brooks will be behind us.

"Two . . ."

The never-ending autumn will pass.

"One."

We will move on from this eternal November. We will move on.

Mom throws the car in drive and presses hard on the pedal, lurching us forward. Then, just as we're right on top of the ridge of overgrowth and pile of leaves before the crumbled bricks, I see it—the glint of a spike.

"Mom, STOP!"

The *pop* is so loud, it echoes through my brain long after Mom has started yelling for us to get out of the car.

"Hurry, they're coming!" she says, pulling Delia and me from our seats, slinging her purse over her shoulder and pushing us toward the hole in the brick wall.

"Quick, it came from over by the wall!" I hear a man's voice echo from the hill.

"Girls, *now*!" Mom says, guiding us as carefully as she can over the debris I can now see was strategically placed over a set of road spikes. "Watch your step," she whispers. Her voice is hoarse, like she wants to scream but her voice is hiding.

"Mom, where are you?" Delia hisses.

I find her hand in the dark and pull my sister close to me. "I've got her," I whisper to Mom, and Mom takes my hand in hers, gripping hard as I keep slipping away. Her palms are sweating so much.

"This way, hurry!" Mom commands, and we follow.

"Over here—I see a car!" a voice hollers. A voice I recognize.

Officer Eve.

They sound too close. I can't find my breath.

"There! The crack in the wall," a different man says. Officer Darryl.

"In here!" Mom hisses, pushing us into a bush thorny enough to carve deep scratches through the fabric of my hoodie. Delia is trembling so much, it shakes me, too. Mom disappears, and at first I think maybe she's going to talk to the police. Normally, she would. Mom's an obsessive rule-follower. I almost stand to pull her back, but then I hear her sink into a nearby bush. She knows we can't outrun them. Now all we can do is make them think we've gone a different way.

Delia's breath begins to speed up. It's getting louder.

"Shhhh," I try to soothe. "In for three, out for four," I say, repeating the advice I got from my therapist. "In for three, out for four."

I press my fingers into her palm, just hard enough for her to focus on the pressure. She eases into my grip, and soon, her breathing begins to slow.

Then, just as the footsteps begin to get closer, they stop.

"Wait," one of the men says. "Do you smell that?"

It's faint at first, the smoky acrid scent of something freshly burnt. But with terrifying speed, the smell grows strong, filling the surrounding air with its toxicity.

"C'mon," says the other man's voice. "If they wanna take their chances out here, let 'em. I can tell you one thing. I'm not."

The set of feet closest to Delia and me stands still for a moment while the others retreat.

"If you're out here," I hear Officer Eve say, her voice low enough to make me think she's looking right at us, inches away, "you won't be for long. Better to just let us find you."

After several more seconds, Officer Eve's boots retreat, too, though, leaving us in the woods alone.

I creep out of the bush first, the thorns taking their toll on the way out. I pull Delia out gingerly and grope for my mom. She finds me first, pulling me into a tight hug before sniffing the air.

"We need to leave," I tell Mom. The panic rising in my chest feels animal. I'm running on pure instinct now.

A twig snaps close by, and we spin to see, but we're completely blind in this part of the woods.

"What is that?" Mom says. "It smells like something is on fire."

"It's nothing good," I say, but for every direction I turn, I swear I smell the burning even more.

"Where's it coming from?" Delia whispers.

"I can't tell."

"Where do we go?"

"I . . . I . . ."

Anywhere. Anywhere but here.

"This way!" I hiss, taking the lead after placing Delia's hand in Mom's.

I keep us close to the wall, dragging my fingers along the brick so I don't take us deeper into the forest and get us lost. We're on the other side of the wall now, but the wooded path leading into Raven Brooks was no less foreboding, as far as I remember. I seem to recall a series of bird incidents.

I want to keep touching brick, but soon, the overgrowth

pushes me away from it, and I lead us into a bramble so thick, I have to swat low-hanging branches every two feet.

"Maybe we should turn back," Mom says.

I'm just about to tell her she's right when I swat one more branch away, and we break into a small clearing.

The light from the moon is dim at best, and I can barely see Delia and Mom behind me. I'm grateful to be out of the overgrowth, but now I've brought us into the open. Now I feel a little like a sitting duck.

Suddenly, the smell of burning is so pungent, my throat starts to burn.

"Piper," I hear Delia whisper behind me, but I already see it.

The tall, stooped shadow, the face molded into a hooked beak, the strands of feathers hanging limp from its grotesquely long limbs.

It takes a step toward us from its place between the shadows on the other side of the clearing.

Then the strangest thing happens. I close my eyes hard and open them again, just to be sure I've seen it. It's almost as though the beak has disappeared, and in its place is a strange, twisted horn. A double-sided horn. No, not a horn—a mustache.

Another step forward, and the beak returns, and this time, to my horror, I see it raise its giant limbs, the full display of its feathers in view.

It tilts its head back, beak to the sky, and to my utter horror, its beak opens. From it emerges a huge puff of white smoke. And the loudest, most primal scream I've ever heard.

Caw! Caw!

CHAPTER 12

"Run!"

I barely get the word out before I'm pushing Mom and Delia back into the thick of the forest, back toward the wall and our broken-down car. I don't know about you, but I'd rather fly right into the hands of the Raven Brooks police than get scooped up by whatever that was. Better be questioned than dead.

Branches slap my face and arms as I try to keep my head low.

I hit the wall too fast and drag my knuckles across the rough brick, but I can hardly feel the burn of it. I'm just relieved to have found it at all. If it's possible, the night has turned even darker.

"Is it behind us?" Delia wheezes.

"Just keep going," I say. I don't dare look back.

But the smell of burning still lingers.

Ahead, I spot the halo of light illuminating the work site.

"Keep going!" I pant, and Mom parts branch after branch to clear the path.

Finally, we reached the tiny crumbled opening in the wall. We clamber over it, gulping for air as we finally chance a glance backward.

I can't see the shadow anymore. I can't smell anything, but that might just be because I'm having trouble breathing.

By some stroke of luck, our car has been left alone, the workers and police still preoccupied looking for their missing person at the top of the hill.

"What now?" I ask Mom, and I hope maybe she has an idea, but soon realize there isn't a look of inspiration on her face. It's a look of dread.

Light illuminates the brush underneath our feet, and I hear the rumble of a familiar engine.

It's the truck.

It bears down on us fast, scraping the edge of the wall with its side mirror and flicking sparks as it squeezes through what barely allowed our car to get by.

About five yards from where we stand, the truck sighs to a stop, but its engine continues growling. The headlights are blinding, and when I squint my eyes open the tiniest bit, I see a large figure swing the door open and climb down fast from the driver's side.

"Stay back!" Mom commands the figure over the engine, spreading her arms like low wings in front of Delia and me.

Whatever it is doesn't listen. It walks toward us so fast, and we all huddle together like one shield. I think it'll have to go through all *three* of us to get to one. That Tillman resilience.

I want so badly to scream, but no call for help could be heard over the rumble of that engine and the shouts of the workers searching for their own.

When the driver moves to the side of his headlights, I finally see it for what it is.

A teenager.

"Get in!" the teenager commands.

"Not a chance," Mom says.

The kid looks shocked. "Would you rather stay out here?"

When we don't answer, he sighs impatiently.

"I'm Jordy," he says, like that should mean something. When he realizes it doesn't, he adds, "Jess's brother?"

I see it now. The giant brown eyes. The intense stare. He's wearing a silver chain around his neck that looks like an identical match to Jess's, at least from what I can see of it; most of it disappears under his shirt collar.

"It's okay," I tell Mom, mostly sure I'm right.

Mom's torn. It's only when she glances at the opening in the wall that she seems to recall what we were just running from.

"Okay," she says, ushering us toward the cab of Jordy's truck. Now that I see it up close, I understand what the huge rumbling engine is for. It's a tow truck. The hook on the back swings under the vibration. An E&J Motors logo takes up most of the door's panel.

"How are we gonna turn around?" I ask once we're squeezed shoulder to shoulder in the vehicle. I'm closest to Jordy, who has to lift his big arm over my head and push my headrest forward just to see behind him. I try not to breathe in too much because I'm inches from his armpit, and he's a teen boy, so you already know what that smells like.

"We aren't," he says, and before I can ask any other questions, he throws the truck in reverse.

"What if they follow us?" I ask, watching the workers on their hill. If they see us, I can't tell from this distance.

"They might," Jordy says, still looking over his shoulder as we push past trees and wall in reverse, branches dragging along the metal at earsplitting rates.

Delia's on to bigger things. Literally.

"The thing in the forest," she says, her voice hoarse with the strain of running. "It wanted to hurt us."

"If it wanted you hurt, you'd be hurt," Jordy replies.

I look up at his face. His square jaw is set in concentration. It's hard to believe he's Mari's nephew with the way he's speaking to us.

"You're not very good at the whole comforting thing," I say.

"Maybe not, but I *am* good at the whole driving thing," he says. "And *doubly* good at showing up when you need someone to drive."

Fair.

Mom hasn't said a word. She's just staring ahead at the work site, frozen, like she can't believe her luck.

Finally, we reach the street back to Raven Brooks. Jordy

drives toward a cluster of houses and low buildings in a part of town I haven't yet seen.

I look at every house and imagine the people sitting inside each one. What are they doing? Do they do the same thing every time the town's been reset?

Mom, seeming to think about the people in the houses, too, says, "No one wants us here." It breaks our uneasy silence. Then she adds, "But no one will let us leave."

I massage my own pressure point on the inside of my palm now. I'm tense—obviously. And Mom's said what I've been thinking for days.

"See, that's where I think you're wrong," Jordy says just as quietly.

This piques Mom's interest. She looks directly at Jordy for the first time since we piled into his truck. "You know how we can get out?"

Jordy shakes his head. "No. You're stuck here, that's for sure."

Mom stops looking at him, and I watch her struggle to swallow something down.

"But I think you're wrong that no one wants you here," he says, this time very carefully. "I think someone wants you here very much."

* * *

Jordy drives us to the E&J Motors headquarters. Or so he calls it. It's really more like a dump. But a happy dump, somehow.

170

Even at night, with its car lifts and tool lockers and oil rags casting shadows across the harsh lights of the buzzing neon above, the place feels like someone has seen it grow from a pile of bricks to a shop that's heard a thousand jokes, smelled hundreds of veggie delight subs, and laid to rest only the sickest of cars that it has treated.

If his sister, Jess, is cryptic, Jordy is nothing of the sort. Not anymore, anyway. He gives us the whole rundown of the place.

"Dad started building E&J Motors when I was four. Jess was only a baby. Dad said he always thought he'd be a journalist like his dad, my gramps, but then he met this friend who was into gadgets and tinkering, and that kind of put him on a new path." He scratches his head. "Dad used to tell me that journalism and car tinkering was really similar. You're just trying to get to the root of the problem. The root of the story, the root of the motor, the root of it all. He was never happy unless he had answers. So fixing cars made him really happy."

Huh. I guess I'd never thought about cars that way.

Jordy wipes down the counter in the corner of the shop. He's already cleared off three metal stools with red vinyl cushions for us. Behind the counter stands a water cooler with one of those giant water jugs turned upside down. When he fills three paper cups for us, the water glubs in the bottle, the sound echoing through the garage.

When I follow the sound upward, I see there's a loft situated at the back of the shop, accessed by a narrow staircase pushed against the wall. A lamplight from inside the loft offers a small peek of the back of a sofa, a television, and a tiny kitchenette.

That's when I realize. This isn't just where Jordy and his dad worked; it's also where Jordy *lives*.

"How old are you?" I ask. Jordy looks at me like it's a weird question. Maybe it is, but I just feel like I need to know.

"Seventeen," he says.

"Your aunt is cool with you living here by yourself?" I ask.

Jordy shrugs. "She's got her hands full with Jess. Besides, it's more like . . . housesitting . . . for Dad. I do pop over to her place for dinner, though."

He pulls up a wheel-y stool from beside one of the car lifts and looks at the three of us for a second before picking a place on the concrete floor to stare at.

"How'd you know where to find us?" asks Delia, gripping her paper cup with both hands.

"I didn't," he says, not taking his eyes off the concrete. "I was following the Crow."

Five days ago, I might have wondered what Jordy meant. Three days ago was a different lifetime. Now? Who knows.

"So, we were just lucky?" asks Delia.

Jordy looks up at her, laughing gently. "Do you feel lucky?"

Delia's lips turn up in the tiniest smile, and I feel genuine gratitude for Jordy. He put my sister at ease. Even for a second, he made her smile.

"Is that what you were doing when you chased me into the woods that day?" I ask.

I don't mean for it to sound so sinister, but Jordy tenses up, and my mom looks ready to fly off her stool.

"When you *what*?"

"I didn't chase you," Jordy says, then turns quickly to my mom. "I didn't chase her."

"You saw the bird man," I say.

Jordy turns to the side, so I see his profile. Then he nods somberly. "I smelled it."

"The burning," I reply. "Why would you risk going after that . . . that *thing*?" I can't even begin to fathom what would compel someone to follow it.

Jordy's jaw sets again. "That *thing* has my father," he says solemnly.

My head feels like it's spinning. I take another sip of water.

"Wait," I say, trying to replay the dinner with Jess and Vinod and Mari. It feels like it was years ago, not hours. "I thought the theory was . . . Mr. Peterson has your dad?"

Jordy stands up fast, sending his stool rolling, and begins to pace the floor. "Peterson," he says, as if it's the first time he tastes that name, ever. "If that's what Jess wants to believe, then fine. Aunt Mari and I know the truth, though."

"Okay," I say, doing my best to gather my scattered thoughts, but my nerves are frayed, and my head is pounding and my arms and legs sting from all the tiny scratches the forest made.

"So, you think this Crow thingy took your dad—"

"I know it did," says Jordy, stopping his pacing to correct me.

"But why?" I ask.

Jordy stares hard at me. "Because my dad had something it wanted."

"What was it?"

Jordy sighs. "I don't know."

"So then how can you be so sure it was the Crow and not Mr. Peterson?" Delia asks.

"Because I was on the phone when he . . ." Jordy starts, his voice catching. He clears his throat and starts again. "I was on the phone when he told me he smelled something burning. That day. In November. He ran down to the shop to make sure it was okay."

A chill passes through me as I remember that first evening at the apartment, the certainty I felt that fire was close enough to singe me. How sure I'd been that I was being watched.

Jordy doesn't need to tell me what happened next. I've put the pieces together.

"The days started resetting after your dad went missing," I say to Jordy as gently as possible.

I glance at Mom, who has been weirdly quiet ever since we got in Jordy's truck. Weirder still is that she hasn't even flinched at the mention of *time resetting itself.* It's like she's witnessing this entire conversation from another dimension.

Jordy brings me back to the question I haven't asked yet.

"I don't know it all yet," he says. "But I do know this is one of the pieces."

Then he reaches for his neck and threads a finger under the sturdy silver chain hanging around it. When he pulls, the charm on the end appears and lands on the outside of his gray T-shirt.

I've seen one like it before.

"Dad never gave up his investigative journalism hobby," he says, holding the medallion on his chain in the palm of his hand. The tiny jewel chip at its center is purple instead of red. Other than that, it's an exact replica of the key ring Cousin Marcia left for my mom.

Now is when I need Mom to join the conversation, but she's still completely in her own world. It's like she's working on a different puzzle from us, in the same room but piecing together an entirely different landscape.

"Mom," I coax, wanting her to show Jordy the key ring. But she acts like she's already resolved that part, moved past it somehow.

She glances at me briefly, nods, and says, "I know, Pip."

She's so quiet, so breathless, I think there might be something really wrong. Even more wrong than the utter backwardness of the last few days.

Jordy is watching this whole thing, eyeing my mom hard.

"You have one, too, don't you?" he asks.

Mom eyes Jordy closely but doesn't answer. Instead, she questions, "What would it mean if I did?"

Jordy doesn't blink. "It would mean you'd be like us," he replies. "Like my sister and my aunt Maritza and Vinod. It would mean that time wouldn't restart for you."

"She doesn't know about the time—" I start, but Mom stops me.

"I do," she says.

"But how—"

"Tell me," she says to Jordy, holding my millions of questions at bay. "Is that thing around your neck a blessing . . . or is it a curse?"

Jordy holds the medallion tighter in his hand and stares so hard at my mom, I think maybe part of their conversation is happening telepathically. I mean, it wouldn't be the strangest part of this night.

"I don't know," he says.

"Mom," Delia interjects, bending the edges of her paper cup compulsively. "What happened to you tonight?"

It happens so seamlessly; I might have missed it if I'd blinked. It's as though this cloud around Mom passed right over her eyes, obscuring her for an instant before dissipating completely, returning the real Mom to us, like the other had been an imposter. Here was Mom again, face creased with worry and fatigue, eyes that can cut through the surface of any exterior, a smile that can make you believe even the most terrifying night will come to an end soon.

"Nothing that can't be undone," Mom says to Delia, wrapping her into a tight hug.

I see Jordy stiffen, but he doesn't say anything. Whatever Mom knows and isn't saying is making him nervous. I know how he feels.

Delia pulls her head from Mom's chest long enough to make a confession. "The police think we had something to do with your dad's disappearance," she says to Jordy, her voice one giant apology for something we didn't do.

Jordy waves off the claim. "They just don't know how to

admit they're clueless. Darryl Stokes will stop asking questions the minute you start feeding him."

Delia giggles. "He likes tacos."

"What?" Jordy says, crestfallen. "I missed tacos night?"

It's the first time since meeting him tonight that Jordy acts like an actual seventeen-year-old kid.

Maybe Jordy and I aren't so dissimilar. For three weeks after Dad died, I slept on the floor of my parents' room. I didn't even ask if I could; I just waited until Mom had fallen asleep. Some nights it took forever. And when she was finally out, I would drag my comforter from my bed and lay it on the floor next to where my dad's side of the bed had always been.

My mom would find me there and coax me back to my room to finish out the night, but I was always glad for whatever time I got on that patch of floor. It was as close as I dared to get. I wouldn't lay in the bed where he used to sleep. I wouldn't pull the shirts from his dresser beside me and bring them up to my face, just so I could smell them and remember how the detergent lingered on the fabric. This was before I shaved my hair, so I always got a whiff of my shampoo, too, but it didn't matter. But on the floor, I could hover right where he used to be. I could exist where he walked. It was just close enough.

I would bet everything I have that Jordy

sleeps on that little couch in the living room I can see from this spot in the garage. I would wager it all and say that he uses paper plates instead of dishes because he wouldn't dare disturb the plates in the cabinet. That when he says he's "housesitting" for his dad, he's really just trying to be as close to him as possible.

There is one big difference, though. Jordy has no idea if his dad will come back. Mine can't.

Mom seems to sense what I'm thinking.

"Why don't you come and stay with us?" she asks, though it's more like a recommendation than an offer. "We don't have much, but the couch is decently comfortable. And we do have unlimited—er, natural groceries." She smiles at her own joke.

Jordy looks taken aback. He fiddles with his hands awkwardly.

"I'm okay here."

"I don't doubt that," Mom says, her voice steady and soft. "But honestly, I think you could use some company."

"I have Aunt Mari," Jordy says, his stiff demeanor softening. "And Jess. They're a text message away." Then he allows himself one small smile. "They don't like it that I'm here, either."

Mom smiles back, her eyes crinkling at the corners like they do when she likes someone. It's the only way to really tell with Mom.

Then, with a technical proficiency that confounds me, Mom pulls out her phone and Raven Brooks–drops her contact information into Jordy's phone. I have to admit it. I'm impressed she knew how to do that.

"Now we're just a text away, too."

She and Jordy share a wordless exchange you can only share with a person you've been through an extraordinary adventure with.

When Jordy drives us home, he says he'll return to the woods for our car. Mom makes him promise to wait until the morning, and they'll go together. I have to hand it to her. She's insistent, and won't take no for an answer.

As Delia and I pile into our bedroom, I'm 100 percent positive that the events of the night will haunt me with every breath. I have zero doubt that the questions and doubts and fears and hopelessness will rattle my brain so hard, I'll have no choice but to stare at the ceiling of Delia's and my room all night.

Yet somehow, I don't remember getting home. I don't remember taking off my shoes or putting myself in bed wearing the same clothes I wore that night. All I remember is floating through the air, the chain of a medallion clinking close to my ear, the sound of my mom's voice . . .

When I wake the next morning, though, the questions are still there.

And the day is November 2.

Again.

CHAPTER 13

"Happy Reset Day?" chirps Delia as we both sit up in bed, staring at our phones like somehow that will catapult us forward in time again.

"You know, I was holding out hope that maybe it just . . . wouldn't happen," I admit. "Like maybe it was all a huge mistake, and Jess and everyone else were . . ."

"Bluffing," says Delia. "Yeah, I know what you mean. How great would it be if it were all just a huge goof? Like, gotcha! What chumps! Can't believe you fell for it! Welcome to the neighborhood."

"It's weird to be wishing for a lie," I say.

Delia and I scurry out of bed, our tummies rumbling for some breakfast. We may have already eaten breakfast on November 2 twice already, but we definitely want it again. Mom isn't in the kitchen, though. Instead, there's a note taped to the door:

Girls—
Went to get the car with Jordy.
DO. NOT. LEAVE. THE. APARTMENT. If you do, I will ground you for the rest of my life, and when I die, I will continue to haunt you as a ghost.

Love,
Mom
P.S.: It's November 2nd. Happy Reset Day.

"Welp," I say, "I hope you like staring at walls because that's all we'll be doing today."

Delia frowns, then immediately lights up.

"The store! That's still technically not leaving the apartment!"

"You want to hang out in the store? The moldy, boarded-up, sad little store we haven't had a chance to clean because we've been too busy trying to figure out why this town is so messed up? That store?"

Delia nods excitedly.

"Gosh," I say, pulling on my clothes for the day. "Sounds tempting, but I'm going to go with wall staring."

Delia sidles closer to me. "*Piper.* We need to look for more spy cams, remember?"

I sigh. It's really, really hard to say no to Delia.

"Uh-oh," Delia says, staring at the dish by the front door. "Mom took the key."

I look in the dish, and while the key is missing, something in the bowl catches the light from the lamp. I pinch it between my fingers and hold it up.

It's the tiny ruby chip from the center of the key chain.

"It must have fallen out," says Delia.

"It's even smaller out of its setting," I reply, eyeing the stone closely. The size isn't the only thing about it that strikes me. I expect to see a stone with smooth, even sides that constitute the plains of the stone. Instead, the rock is more like a chip, a piece of something larger.

Something that's been smashed to bits.

"Now how are we going to get into the store?" mopes Delia.

I remember the passage from the kitchen.

"There's always Spider Alley," I say.

Delia backs away.

"Not a chance."

"C'mon," I say. "*You're* the one who wanted to find some hidden surveillance. How bad do you want to do it? Huh?"

Okay, I'm baiting my sister. But really, Mom can't get too mad at us for going to the store. Our old house was two floors anyway, so this is really just like that. Plus, the store's locked, and we're not going anywhere unsafe or that she can't get to.

See? I deserve a "Daughter of the Year" award.

I'll settle for a "Daughter of November 2" award, though. Sorry, Delia.

Delia steels herself. "Okay," she says, puffing up her chest. "If you're so brave, go for it, Lady Arachnid."

I like a good challenge, even if I hate, and I mean *hate*, spiders. But I have a few tricks up my sleeve. Or should I say, web. I reach under the kitchen counter and flip the hidden switch, popping the door open just a crack. I ease myself through the crack, and without pulling the chain to the bulb above, take two steps in, keeping the door partially closed behind me.

"It's not bad at all, you big scaredy-cat. Nothing but a few—"

I go quiet. And wait . . .

"Pip? What is it? Pip? Pip? Pip?"

"Nothing, just . . . ouch!"

I slap the wall. Then I slap it harder, enough to make a ruckus.

"Ow! Oh . . . oh my g—Delia, they're everywhere!"

"Pip!"

I slap and yelp and slap again.

"They're—they're taking me down, Delia, *help*! They're all over me!"

"Pip!"

"They're—giving me . . ." I pause. "They're giving me . . . Ahhh! Radioactive powers! I'm becoming . . . impervious to woodchucks!"

Silence. Then.

"I hate you," Delia says.

I can't stop. "No longer will I live in fear of the rabid bite of the woodchuck!"

I swing the door open, cackling, then pull the chain above my head to light the bulb.

"I think Mom did some exterminating," I explain. "All clear."

Delia shoves past me.

"I *really* hate you," she says.

"Well, you'll *really* love me during the next woodchuck invasion."

"I didn't even have woodchuck invasion on my Raven Brooks bingo card," Delia replies.

I want to stay in that place where I was laughing. For just that second, it wasn't Reset Day, it was just Delia and me, and I was getting her back for pranking me, and she was already plotting her vengeance. Mom was out, and we were teaming up to figure out how to bend the rules without breaking them.

But once I scan the shelves in the dark, musty aisles of the Natural Grocer, I'm reminded of all the ways I thought this store was supposed to be our new beginning. I remember how much we wanted to believe we were starting over. The three of us were a new team, Delia and Mom and me, forging our way into a new life without Dad. There were no unexplained earthquakes, boarded-up houses with ghosts still lurking, the burnt remains of an amusement park that should never have been built, ciphers so complicated not even someone with all the repeating days in the world could solve, and Crows that stalk their prey and make them disappear.

This store is not our new beginning. That much is obvious. Neither is what Marcia Tillman left us. Our new beginning is Reset Day, the moment when time folds in on itself and repeats, making everyone relive the same days over and over, except for a select handful of people.

People who hold a piece of something bigger.

People, as Jordy implied, who are meant to be here.

Instead of coming to a new life, we've sunk ourselves into a world that refuses to let us move on.

I guess it's time we face facts.

"What do you think a 'Norman's Navel' is?" Delia asks, rounding the

RAVEN BROOKS

B I N G O

Crows	Ravens	Angry Mob	Mr. Dork
Mushroom Kale Salad	Officer Eve	Officer Darryl	Reset Day
The Food Barn	November	Spiders	Enzo Missing
The Billboard	Woodchuck Invasion		

corner of my aisle while rattling an orange package of clinking glazed disks.

"Um, either some sort of citrus candy or something that came out of some dude named Norman's navel," I reply.

Delia shoves the package into the shelf closest to her.

"Not worth the risk," she says.

Our search for anything remotely hidden or spy cam–ish is unsuccessful. We try instead to look for candy that hasn't gone completely stale (I keep wishing that I'd saved more of my fruit leathers), but that search is just as disappointing.

I get the sense that Delia is as disillusioned as I am because we're largely silent as we come to the conclusion that the store is, in a word, hopeless.

"I'll call it," I say so Delia doesn't have to be the one to do it. "It's a bust. No good can come of this store."

"Don't let Mom hear you say that," Delia says.

"I'm pretty sure Mom already knows," I reply.

We begin dragging ourselves up the stairs, when the middle bit of the staircase confuses my footing.

For some reason, it didn't mess me up on the way down, but on the way back up, I notice that the steps between the seventh and eighth are completely uneven. It's like there should be an extra step in between.

"What's going on here?" I ask, stretching my leg to hoist myself up to the ninth step.

"Maybe they ran out of wood when they were building," guesses Delia, but now she's looking at the abnormal steps, too.

"It's almost like . . ." I start to say, but my hand slips on the dust and my elbow slides out from under my weight, crashing into the panel beside the stairs that should be a wall.

Should be, but isn't.

"Are you okay?" Delia asks once the dust clears. She's only half paying attention to me rubbing my elbow that hurts bad enough for me to think I'll never straighten it again.

I understand in a second, though, when I see her crouched beside the hole I've made in the panel.

"Move your head," I instruct, nudging her over enough for me to be able to see what she's seeing.

And what she's seeing is a room. A full-width, half-height room.

I cough on the dust we've not only kicked up but unearthed in the secret . . .

"Office?" I wonder, and Delia squints through the dust and dark.

"I hope so," she says. "Because it's either that or a dungeon."

"Yeah, let's go with office," I say, banking on the desk and squat stool I can make out from the meager light offered by the store below.

"Age before beauty," she says, lifting her eyebrow at me.

An oldie but a goodie.

"Fine," I say, definitely not thinking about all the spiders that have probably migrated from the staircase to here. "But if there's treasure in here, I'm keeping all of it."

I can't decide if it's better to crouch or stoop inside the hidden office. Either way is uncomfortable, and neither seems very practical for long.

"How tall was Cousin Marcia again?" Delia says, crawling into the office behind me.

"Taller than this," I reply. "Either the apartment was just built over this place or—"

"Or she wanted it to stay hidden," Delia says.

And judging by everything we've learned about Cousin Marcia, I'm going with the latter.

A quick survey of the secret office reveals almost nothing. There's the desk and stool, which I can now see have been purposely chopped down at the legs.

Okay, so that pretty much settles it. Cousin Marcia wanted to keep this little office a secret.

There's a squat chest of drawers lining one of the walls. When I open three of the drawers, they're full of dust and nothing more. But when I go to open the fourth drawer, it's locked.

"Of course it is," I grumble.

"Look over here," Delia says, sifting through the stacks of papers left on the desk. "Some are pretty recent."

It's mostly bills and maintenance receipts for the store's operations, each stamped with angry red *FINAL NOTICE* warnings and coated with a thin layer of dust. Every single piece of paper dates back to November 1 or earlier. Like everywhere else in Raven Brooks, time in the Natural Grocer's half office stopped advancing on Reset Day.

I turn in my crouch slowly, wanting to make sure I'm not

missing a single thing in this weird little hidden room where Marcia conducted her business. Then my eyes land on the treasure.

"No. Way."

"What?" Delia asks, scooting in my direction. "What? I don't see anything!"

I rush to the corner of the room, scraping my knees along the old hardwood floor, tearing my jeans just a little more. It doesn't matter, though. There, buried under a small mountain of manila folders and old receipts, is a genuine ListenBetterXE350. The first-of-its-kind multi-input audio receiver/adjuster, complete with original headphones and studio microphone.

"I think maybe Marcia didn't know how cool she was," I say.

"Or you don't know how dorky you are," Delia replies.

I glare at her. "Don't be jealous because you don't know good vintage."

"I collect vinyl," Delia hisses. "Of course I know good vintage."

I marvel at the old technology, with its dials and analog and red-needled level controls.

"Why would she have this?" I ask myself more than Delia, but she answers anyway.

"Maybe for store announcements or something?"

I try flipping a couple of the switches, but I can't get any power to the receiver.

I deflate a little. "I guess it was too much to hope it would still work."

"Bummer," says Delia. "Guess you'll have to go and buy your junk from a garage sale or something."

I barely have time to send another glare in her direction before I notice something strange attached to one of the inputs.

"Odd," I say, trying to pull out the cable.

"Yes, you are," says Delia.

I smack her shoulder without even looking. I'm that good.

But then I notice something. It's been modified. I try jiggling the cord a little, and the receiver tries to spark to life. Tiny static sounds crackle underneath the equipment.

"Maybe if I just hold this in place," I mutter, squeezing a clamp around a different cord a little bit tighter.

Suddenly, the hidden office is alive with the sound of . . .

"Farts?" Delia laughs.

"Ohmygosh, I can almost smell the gas it's so bad," I say between gasps for air. It sounds like two kids. Whoever are making the sounds on the recording are cracking up even harder than we are.

"I call this one the Deadly Nightshade," one of the boys on the recording says, and a high, whiny fart fills the room. Delia is on her back, rolling like a beetle.

"Aaron, Aaron!" says the other voice. "Deadly Nightshade, meet the Silent Killer!"

Suppressed giggles fill the space of the recording, and all I can hear after that is wheezing.

"Oh man, I think I'm gonna puke," says the boy called Aaron. "Nicky for the win."

Nicky. Aaron. Where have I seen those names before . . . ?

Then it rushes back to me. The fence along the llama farm.

It's the strangest feeling, hearing voices (and farts) connected to the names I traced my finger across on those old slats of wood. It's yet another place our paths have intersected in this strange new world. I find myself wishing for just a second with these two boys who laugh at the things we laugh at. I picture sitting down with them at our cramped little breakfast nook, fighting over a single, precious fruit leather discovered buried in a cabinet, right next to the place where Mom discovered the disabled spy cam.

I wonder if I would ask them all the questions that I have.

Or maybe I'd just eat with them. It would be nice to just eat with a friend and not think of anything other than what food tastes like.

I barely have time to imagine what that might be like before the sound of the boys' laughter cuts out, and in its place, I hear a different voice. A woman's voice.

There's no other way to describe it; the voice is shrill. It's the type of voice no one would want to listen to for long. Which makes me almost certain that it's Marcia on the recording.

"Testing, testing," says the voice, sitting close enough to the mic for me to hear every pop and crackle. I turn the volume down to shield my ears, but now I have to lean into the speaker to hear her when she talks.

"Today is . . . let's see. Real world: March thirty-first. Raven Brooks world: November twentieth. Found and dismantled another device today. Location: living room air-conditioning vent. Device: hidden camera or recording device. Presence of burning odor for . . . let's see . . . thirty seconds yesterday.

Direction: northeast of the west forest entrance, best as I could tell."

I can hear notepaper crinkling in the background, like she's checking notes. And I hate to admit it, but the way she crinkles the paper is like how I brush through my school binders. *Same hands.*

Then the recording grows quiet, the only sound the presence of static, before Marcia's voice creeps back in, quieter this time. "I know he's watching me."

A gasp slips out before I can catch it, but Delia heard. It doesn't matter. She's as uncomfortable as I am.

Cousin Marcia continues: "The pieces must all be found. The ones who hold them hold the last defense."

I look up at the same time Delia does. We're trying to stare a hole through the ceiling into the bowl by the door. The one that holds the piece of whatever Marcia is talking about. The piece of stone that came from Mom's key ring.

Static overtakes the recording again, and I think maybe we've heard the end of it. Then, just as I'm about to switch it off, we hear her voice one more time.

"More will go missing if we can't restore the clock."

The tape ends with a loud crack, its tail running out on its reel with a *pop.*

I switch off the receiver so fast, I rock the box on its heels, letting it come back down to the floor in a puff of smoke.

I look at Delia, finding her in the thick silence.

"She was paranoid," I say, trying to explain away the last

sentence Cousin Marcia uttered before the recording stopped. "Who knows how much of that was even real?"

Delia looks at me, deadly serious, and in this moment I'm positive she's no longer young enough to be lied to. "All of it is real."

I reach for her ankle because that's all I can find in the darkness that's started to settle in the hidden room. "I know."

We replace the broken board with a new panel we find in the corner of the office and prop it in place to hide the damage we did to the original panel beside the staircase.

Inside the apartment, Delia and I are quiet for a long time while we consider the vague warnings Cousin Marcia deemed important enough to record and dangerous enough to say in code. I stare at the piles of books and photocopies on the coffee table, dog-eared and flagged with all the Post-its and margin notes my mom managed to scrawl before rushing off to the meeting that led to our living nightmare last night.

It's grown dark in the apartment before I crawl out of my fog long enough to notice how quiet it still is.

"Shouldn't Mom be back by now?" I ask Delia, who has been occupying her own fog for half the evening. My angry stomach alerts me to the fact that we somehow managed to sail right past lunch and have moved into dinner.

The screen on my phone reads five thirty in the evening. Which would explain why the dark has begun to overtake the sky.

"Maybe she decided to wait at Jordy's?" Delia suggests, but I can tell she's about as convinced as I am.

I look at my phone again, searching for messages or texts from either of them.

"Did she tell you anything about being late?" I ask.

Delia shakes her head, getting the same crease between her eyes that Mom gets when she's worried.

I pull the note from its taped place on the door and read it for a second time. Then a third.

Nothing about her being this late.

I snatch my phone from the table and message Jordy at the number he gave us, taking a deep breath to steady my shaking fingers.

She's just running late, I tell myself.

She's just waiting at Jordy's shop while the car gets fixed.

I steady my thumbs to type.

Hey can you tell my mom to call me?

I hit send and stare at the screen, waiting for the telltale dots to let me know he's responding. My heart slows when I finally see them.

It stops altogether when the message appears.

What do you mean? She went home five hours ago!

I drop the phone because I can't feel my hands.

"Pip!" Delia says, picking up the phone where it lands.

She looks to me for answers. She looks to me for anything that says she's wrong. Her fears are unfounded. But I can't fake it.

Everything in me knows that something is horribly wrong. Mom should have been home hours ago.

Then, before I can fully recover from Jordy's message, another lights the screen.

Only this one isn't from Jordy.

There, beside the icon of the shadowed Crow, its sinister

outline lurking on the phone's screen beside the text, reads a message that opens a new gate of terror in my heart:

Where will you run now, little rabbit?

. . .

She's gone.

And there's something else. The image of a man on my screen. With a mustache . . .

About the Author

CARLY ANNE WEST is the author of the YA novels *The Murmurings* and *The Bargaining*. She holds an MFA in English and Writing from Mills College and lives with her husband and two kids near Portland, Oregon. Visit her at carlyannewest.com.